THREAT FROM THE NORTH

A VIKING WITCH MYSTERY

CATE MARTIN

Cover design by Shezaad Sudar.

Rune art by BettyStrange at Dreamstime.com.

Ratatoskr Press logo by Aidan Vincent Kise.

ISBN 978-1-965167-29-8

❊ Formatted with Vellum

CHAPTER ONE

Sometimes, it feels like the whole world is holding its breath, waiting for something that's about to happen.

Maybe I felt that more acutely this October because I was alone with my six-toed black cat Mjolner, winterizing my cabin out in the woods far from the crowds of my hometown of Villmark. The cabin was in a hollow between taller hills, too far to catch any of the breezes blowing in from Lake Superior. The air there was often still, little more than a stirring of the tallest branches of the trees around me.

And yet, this October was even quieter than usual. An early frost had killed the last of the mosquitoes, and it was far too late in the year for them to return after the weather warmed back to making sweaters or jackets unnecessary to be comfortable outdoors. The native animals were surely still about in their burrows and nests. But they were strangely subdued.

Yeah. It was exactly like everything in the woods around me was holding its breath. Waiting.

But it was early October. Winter wasn't exactly looming yet. Even the gales of November were a month away.

And I remembered how jumpy I had been the year before, my first fall on the North Shore. My grandmother had teased me for my nervousness at the approach of winter. And she had been right. I had survived the winter just fine.

I mean, I had survived *the weather* just fine. Other things had proved far more threatening. Like love-struck young women. Lust-struck young men.

The Wild Hunt. The illustrator in me may have wanted to see the Wild Hunt up close for artistic reference purposes, but the rest of me never needed to be that close to anything that soaked in supernatural eek ever again.

And then there was Solvi, the man who had left me the cabin I was now securing the shutters over the windows of. Although, in his defense, as much as he had killed a man, he hadn't ever threatened me. He had just chosen self-exile for his crime, walking off into the north to never return.

That had only been the second murder I had investigated using my newfound powers of Nordic magic. And it had been a shock to realize that Solvi, a man who had blood on his hands, had also used those hands to create so much wondrous beauty.

His lonely cabin in the woods was truly a work of art. Every beam was carved in intricate knotwork patterns. The bed frame carvings told the story of the founding of Villmark in intricate detail. And, best of all, the central pillar that supported the cabin's roof was an elaborate wood sculpture of Yggdrasil, the world tree, complete with the squirrel Ratatoskr in its branches running between the eagle on top and the dragon curled by the roots that disappeared through gaps in the floorboards.

But he had. He had used his artist's hands to take another life. I knew his reasons. But I would still never *understand* why he did it.

Well, all of that had happened over the months of the last winter. Given the way life seemed to come at me now that I was the appointed volva—a sort of Nordic witch—since my grandmother had stepped down from the role, I doubted this winter would be any less eventful.

But I was sure I would get through it just fine. And I wasn't remotely worried about the weather. Cold I could handle. Snow and ice? No problem.

So why was this breath-holding feeling creeping me out so much?

I bolted shut the last of the shutters, then went back inside the cabin for one last poke through the kitchen cupboards. I didn't want to leave something behind that would make for a nasty surprise when I returned in the spring.

Mjolner was stretched out on the bare mattress of the bed, paws spread wide and toes even wider, as if I had just caught him in mid-yawn. Then he winked one yellow-green eye at me quizzically.

"Almost done," I said to his unspoken question.

He made a sound somewhere between a meow and a purr. What that meant, I didn't have a clue.

My friend Loke would've known, though. If he hadn't gone to the north months before. Taking my boyfriend Thorbjorn with him. Unlike Solvi, they were supposed to be coming back. And every week that passed when they didn't, my worry deepened.

But for once, it wasn't the biggest worry weighing on my mind. No, that would be the new duty I was set to begin the next day.

Advising the council of three during their meetings with the public. I had never had reason to make a public petition to them before, so I had never even seen one of these meetings in action. But the next morning I would be sort of presiding over one. Well, more like observing, but still.

To say I was nervous would be a huge understatement.

I would rather face off against a tribe of ogres again.

Alas, the ogres kept to themselves. The people of Villmark, however, were a community. And communities always had grievances to air. And a need for someone to arbitrate those grievances.

I made one last pass with a cleaning rag around my already spotless kitchen, then picked up my overloaded backpack. I had my inevitable struggle with getting both my arms through the straps, then settled the weight comfortably on my back before taking up my walking stick.

This was new for me, having a permanent walking stick. It had been a gift from my grandmother. I think because she knew I had finally realized that her own stick, which she carried everywhere, was far from just a span of wood.

She had imbued hers with magic. Mine was just ordinary wood, if a particularly sturdy oak that had been rubbed and oiled to bring out all the natural beauty in the wood. She had gotten my close friend and dedicated woodworker Andrew Swanson to make it for me, so really it was a gift from two people who cared for me deeply.

That was a fine start. But until I imbued it with my own magic, it was far from the potent staff my grandmother wielded. And that process, she had told me when she had given mine to me, had taken her decades. To get the best effects, you needed to always carry it with you and let it absorb bits of your magic almost coincidentally, because it was just there when you were working that magic.

So now, like my customary bag of art supplies, I carried it with me everywhere. But it had only been a couple of weeks since I had gotten it. I hadn't done a bit of real magic in that time. Just my usual meditations on the runes.

I slung that art bag across my body so that it rested on my hip, hiked the pack up a little higher on my shoulders, then turned to summon Mjolner.

Who was already off the bed, waiting as expectantly as any dog right at my heel, ready to go.

"Trouble in town?" I asked him.

He meowed, but that meow I *did* understand. It meant no.

Or, I was eighty percent sure it meant no.

I sighed my way through one last pang for Loke and Thorbjorn, then gripped my walking stick and headed out of my cabin. I paused to be sure the door latched securely behind me. Then I headed south, following the barest hints of a trail through the woods that would lead me back to Villmark.

"Iss," I said to Mjolner as we walked. "That's the rune I'm working on. It means ice, which we don't have any of currently."

For which I was grateful. It was actually pleasantly warm even under the cover of the evergreen trees and their now bare-branched cousins the beeches and other deciduous trees.

Mjolner made a little meow that I took to mean, "Go on."

"It also means stillness," I told him. "Unchangeability. Like old ice. Like glaciers. Well, climate change aside. Like glaciers were for my ancestors, I guess. Unchanging."

Mjolner made another nudging meow.

"I was just thinking," I said, giving my new walking stick unnecessarily jaunty swings as we walked. Because when its golden surface caught the rare sunbeams that penetrated the canopy, it was really quite a lovely effect. "I was thinking, maybe meditating so much on Iss while we were out here in the woods is why I'm so acutely aware of this feeling, like the world is holding its breath. I've been focusing on stillness. No big surprise if I keep seeing it around me. Right?"

Mjolner didn't respond, but something in the way his head was tipped ever so slightly to the left told me he was thinking hard about his answer.

Then he made a small, almost hesitant mew. And glanced up at me, but only briefly.

I stopped in my tracks. "Mjolner, are you saying you sense it too? That the whole world is waiting? No, the whole world is *bracing* for something? You feel it too?"

He tipped his head and pondered again, then gave another mew. But there was no hesitancy in this one.

"What's coming, Mjolner?"

I supposed he just shook himself off like animals do before resuming our walk home.

But I didn't think that's what it was. I think it was as close as he could get to a shrug.

"You don't know?" I asked as I hurried to catch up with him. I was no longer indulging in jaunty swings of my stick. How could such a little cat keep up such an aggressive pace?

He meowed. Definitely a no, that meow.

"But you're not worried?" I asked. Because that sort of shrug had felt very nonchalant.

He meowed again.

I wanted to say he sounded noncommittal. But I was once more all too aware that I didn't understand him most of the time.

Not that it mattered. Mjolner always looked out for me. I mean, I didn't know what he was, exactly. My sort of honorary grandfather Frór had found him far out in the untamed wilderness north of Villmark, in the lands where ogres, dwarves and alves called home and humans most definitely did not. He had power; I knew that. But what he was? Not even my grandmother had a clue to the answer to that question.

But what was unquestionable was that Mjolner was always there to look out for me. To protect me. He could break spells if he had to. He could walk through walls. He could cover vast distances in the blink of an eye.

So if he wasn't worried, I shouldn't be worried either. And if he was worried, he would already be in full protection mode.

Which, maybe he was. Because, whatever he was on a deeper level, he was still on the surface a cat. And cats were all about conserving effort and energy.

He had been with me all through the last several days when I had been alone at the cabin. He had been mostly napping. Napping and yawning and napping again. Like all the work I was doing was *so* boring to watch.

But he had been there, without fail. And that was a bit unusual. He tended to come and go, wandering as his kitty-cat heart dictated.

Had he been sticking with me because something was worrying him? Or because he simply had nowhere else he had wanted to be?

I couldn't just ask him and hope to get a meaningful answer. But maybe I didn't need to. Because we were heading back to my townhouse in Villmark, the home I currently shared with Loke's sister Esja and with Roarr, the man who looked out for Esja when I wasn't there. If Mjolner had only been staying close to me because I had been alone in the woods far from the reach of my family and friends in an emergency, that wouldn't be true after we got home.

That would be the real test, then. If he stayed with me all through the evening of settling back in to my home in town, sorting laundry and making sure the kitchen was stocked, catching up with my roommates and checking in with my grandmother, that would tell me something.

If he was still there in my bed in the morning, that would really tell me something.

And if he came with me to the council meeting in the morning? Then, maybe I'd allow myself a proper worry.

But in the meantime? In the meantime, sometimes a quiet is just a pleasant quiet to be enjoyed, and not the actual calm before a storm.

I mean, that had to be true, right?

Sometimes?

CHAPTER TWO

As it turned out, I didn't have good testing conditions for my theory. When Mjolner and I finally reached the house in town, it was to find no one there to answer my calls of hello. I left my hiking shoes under the bench by my front door, dropped my art bag and backpack in the living room, then went into the kitchen. The one room in Villmark or in Runde where you were pretty much guaranteed to run into somebody at any hour.

But it was empty, save for a note left on the table, one corner tucked under the butter dish.

Roarr and Esja had gone down to Runde for dinner at my grandmother's mead hall, and would be lingering after, so I shouldn't wait up.

Which was fine. Totally fine. A quiet evening at home to get all those settling in chores done before the council meeting in the morning was just what I needed.

I mean, I had no real reason to fuss over Esja anymore. Sure, when I had first met her, she had been a sickly, housebound girl, thin and pale but always sunny in her disposition. I had called on her as often as I could, as the two of us shared a love of art, if hers was more for watercolors and mine more for the chiaroscuro of charcoal or black ink.

And, yeah, when her brother had gone north in search of answers to the cause of her illness, among other things, I had definitely had a reason to fuss over her. She had been my responsibility, and she had still seemed so frail.

But then, two months ago, things started to change for her. I couldn't be sure, not logically, but my gut was positive that somehow she had become a channel for the Norns. The Norns were Norse goddesses of fate, but aside from both being groups of three, they had very little in common with their Greek or Roman counterparts. They didn't create fate. They just saw it and measured it.

And time for my ancestors wasn't like time for the Greeks either. There was a past, a present, and a future, but to my ancestors, those three concepts were deeply entwined. The future could be seen—at least, by the Norns—because it grew from the past. But the present, the present was just like a single cell from the celluloid print of a feature film. An isolated moment in time. The smallest of things.

And that mattered, because Esja still had one Norn left to channel. But that Norn was Verdande, and her realm was the present. That single moment in time, there and gone in a flash. Such a small thing to fear.

And yet, the present was where we lived, wasn't it?

Still, as scary as her first channelling had been, when Urd, the Norn of the past, had come through her, it had left Esja stronger than it had found her. She had almost summoned pure chaos out of a magical well, but Roarr and I had stopped her in time. And honestly, I still didn't think that had technically been Urd's doing. There was something else at play here, something Roarr could sense but was invisible to me.

But after she had channeled Skuld, the Norn of the future? After that, she had become so easy to mistake for one of the Mikkelsen sisters even at close range. And the Mikkelsen sisters are living valkyries, with the toned arms and acuity with martial weapons to match. Overnight, Esja could leap fences, run long distances without flagging, and even wield a sword or knife as if she had been born with those blades in her hands and had trained with them every day of her twenty-two years since.

To look at her now, there was no sign she had instead spent most of those years as an invalid.

I didn't know what effects channeling Verdande would have on her, but it was hard not to bet they would be positive ones. Or, if they were not, that she didn't already have the strength to meet that challenge and then some.

She wasn't the frail girl that Loke had left behind anymore, that was sure.

And if I was still a little nervous at all the time she spent in the company with Roarr, a man who hadn't killed anyone but who may or may not have aided and abetted a murderer, depending on how much he was really under the influence of controlling magic?

Well, she was also still spending a lot of time with Skefill. And that young man, with his views that no one in Villmark should associate with anything from outside of Villmark—such as me, who despite my long Villmarker lineage had been born in St. Paul, Minnesota—put me far more on edge than Roarr ever could.

Not that Skefill wasn't trying to get along with me currently. Since I had saved his sister and her family the month before, when a predatory entity from the depths of Lake Superior had been hunting in the streets of Villmark, he had taken a far less combative tone with me when our paths crossed. Which, given how much time he spent "weapons training" with Esja, was considerable.

I could only hope that attitude would persist. Because I wasn't the only new element in the morning's council meeting. There was also him and his close friend, Raggi, another isolationist. And I hadn't saved Raggi's family. He still scowled darkly every time he saw me. He might not say a word these days, but his disapproval was palpable.

So that first evening back home, I was as alone as I had been back at the cabin. Mjolner naturally stayed with me, always in my sightline as I moved from room to room unpacking and running load after load of laundry in the machine tucked under the stairs.

Villmark might be kept apart from the modern world, protected behind a magical barrier that not even modern technology with its drones or satellites could penetrate or even perceive was there, but it was not a village trapped in the past. It didn't exactly look like modern Scandinavia, really, but considering my ancestors had arrived on the North Shore way back in the tenth century, why would it? That was a huge amount of time for one split culture to become two distinct things.

And as much as the isolationists might reject things like cellphones and blue jeans infiltrating their sheltered community, no one but the staunchest of zealots wanted to wash their clothes by hand when there was a better option.

And I'm sure it goes without saying, those zealots who want everything done the old way mainly want someone else to do it the old way for them. And seem genuinely perplexed when they all end up terminally single.

I did wonder, briefly as I moved a load from washer to dryer and pushed all the appropriate buttons to get things going, whether Skefill was softening enough to avoid that fate.

But then I pushed all thoughts of him—and Roarr and Esja—from my mind and sat down at my easel to spend a solid hour communing with my new rune before bedtime.

Drawing the rune I was studying over and over again and ruminating on the meaning usually triggered something to awaken in my mind as I slept. Sometimes the insights were so profound it almost felt like I was cheating.

But I had my doubts about this rune. Because Iss was just a single vertical line. Like a capital I with no lines across the top and bottom. And drawing it over and over again felt way too much like the warmups I do to get my hands ready for real art.

Still, I kept at it, Mjolner curled up at my feet, until my hour was up. Then I dumped my toasty warm load of dry clothes into a basket, moved the last load from the washer to the dryer, then carried that basket up to my bedroom.

Nothing nicer than crawling into a bed made with fresh-from-the-dryer sheets wearing equally warm pajamas. I was asleep the instant my head touched the pillow.

It felt like I woke up just as quickly. Like my entire night's sleep was a single blink of my eyes. But my bedroom was now filled with the golden hues of an October sunrise.

And Mjolner was still asleep, curled up against the back of my neck on his two-thirds of my pillow. Typical.

I needed to get going if I was going to reach the council hall before the meeting started, but I took a moment to close my eyes again and try to summon up any fragments of dreams that might linger in my mind. If I didn't catch them now, they would be gone forever. And I *had* intended to dream about the meaning of Iss.

But maybe it was because it truly felt like I had only closed my eyes, then opened them again with nothing in between, but my mind couldn't conjure a single dream image from the night before. Which was strange. I usually dream intensely and extensively every single night. Epic tales that I had to learn from a young age that other people absolutely didn't want to hear a blow-by-blow of.

But all I had, even after concentrating on it, was a vague sense that I had heard a shush-shush sound. Like skis on snow. Cross-country skis shooshing at a brisk pace. But that was it. No visuals. No sensation of cold. No smell of the snow.

"Pretty boring dream," I said out loud.

Mjolner opened a single eye to regard me balefully, then let it slip shut again to resume his slumber.

I probably took too long sorting out my outfit, especially considering I had laid it out the night before. And that I really only had a few outfits that were so thoroughly Villmarker they would be considered appropriate for a council meeting. My grandmother might roll in with jeans and flannel and her hiking boots always caked with mud from the walk up from Runde, but I wanted to make a better impression on my first day.

But clearly the volva outfit my grandmother had given me was too much of an impression. It was lovely—a long dress of alternating panels of red and green with truly voluminous sleeves of snowy white

—but very formal. And as much as I loved the way the green color flattered my red hair and pale, freckled complexion, I really wasn't a long skirts kind of girl.

So what I had left out was really my only option, the outfit I had commissioned myself. It had a similar look to my formal garb with panels of green and red, but was a knee-length tunic over leggings, and without the sleeves that were impossible for me to keep clean. Especially since they were so long they were a tripping hazard.

Even so, I dithered so long over the details of whether to leave my hair loose or braid it, and whether I should braid it into one plait like my grandmother or two like the Mikkelsens, and then brushing it all back out again when I went back to the original loose hair decision, that by the time I was ready to go downstairs I had no time left for breakfast.

Which I knew I was going to regret. Because I had been warned that this would be a long day.

But there was nothing to be done about it now. With a sigh, I headed downstairs. At least the sound of voices in my kitchen heartened me a little. I paused in the kitchen doorway to see Roarr working the stove, making bacon and eggs, while Esja slid freshly sliced bread into the toaster. The two of them were chatting easily with each other about something they had seen the night before. I didn't catch all the details before they saw me standing there and both turned to give me a welcoming smile.

"Can't stay," I said apologetically. "I'm already late. But we'll catch up at dinner?"

"I'll cook," Roarr offered at once. Esja gave him a playful punch in the arm, like he had spoken up faster than she could. Not that I had ever seen her cook before. But Roarr just rubbed at his arm, making a playful show of being hurt.

Then he turned back to the stove to fuss with the bacon, and I saw him shake out that arm as unobtrusively as he could. I would bet she had left a mark. And I would further bet that she didn't realize she had. She didn't know her own strength these days.

"Take some toast, at least," Esja said, pulling hot slices out of the toaster with quick fingers and stacking them on a cloth napkin before thrusting them at me.

"Thanks," I said. What I really needed was coffee, but I could see the coffeemaker on the counter might be filling the air with the aroma of dark roasted beans, but it was very far from being done brewing.

"Mjolner is going with you?" Roarr asked.

Which struck me as a very strange question. Was he turning into some kind of mind-reader?

But then I looked down and saw Mjolner sitting right by my heel. He looked up at me with the strangest look I'd ever seen on a cat.

It was impatience.

And it wasn't about food.

"I guess so," I said, bemused. "And we're late," I added, mostly for the cat's benefit. "I'll see you at dinner."

"Yes," Roarr agreed, moving the cast iron pan off the heat before turning the eggs over to finish cooking.

"Be nice to Skefill, okay?" Esja said. "He's really nervous. And he comes across as grumpy when he's nervous."

I opened my mouth to argue with that overly kind interpretation of his demeanor. But Mjolner made the smallest of mews, and I shut it again with no words said. I just gave her a brisk nod, then headed to the bench by the front door to put on my soft leather Villmarker shoes.

"Your coming," I said to Mjolner in a near whisper, not that I knew who I thought would overhear us or why that would be a problem. "Is that because I'm nervous, or because you're nervous?"

He just blinked at me, but the air of impatience was stronger than ever.

Shoes on, I grabbed my art bag and walking stick, and the two of us headed out into the autumn morning.

CHAPTER THREE

For a moment when I first stepped outside, I had that feeling again. Like the whole world was holding its breath. The air in my front garden was so still, and the golden sunshine just peeking over the fence was warm but almost soporifically so.

But once I had opened my gate and Mjolner and I emerged onto the cobblestone road, that illusion was shattered. We were swept up into the early morning crowd, all heading south, downhill to the marketplace. There was still no breeze to speak of, but the air was definitely moving around because it was filled with the scents of freshly baked bread from the handful of bakeries that were always the first shops to open.

I tapped my walking stick as I walked, exchanging nods and greetings with my fellow Villmarkers, and Mjolner trotted at my side, head held high as if he were some sort of show cat.

Everyone seemed to be in a uniquely good mood. Maybe because of the fine autumn weather that was holding on for longer than anyone could have hoped. I even heard people whistling or humming songs under their breaths, almost like they didn't quite know they were doing it. Just making cheery sounds.

The crowd around us thinned out a bit after we passed the marketplace, replaced with a smaller number of people coming up from the valley to do their shopping. South of the marketplace was mostly farms and open fields, unlike the closely packed residences on the top of the hill.

I was heading to the tallest structure in Villmark, the council meeting hall. The tall crossed beams of its roof were imposing, even though more than half the town was at a higher elevation than it.

It was also the oldest still standing building in Villmark. It didn't quite date back to our original settler ancestors, who had hid for some time in the caves behind the waterfall that was now the division between the hidden town of Villmark and the northern Minnesotan town of Runde that existed in the nonmagical world.

I only knew the vaguest outlines of the history of Villmark, and I really wanted to rectify that. But mastering the runes and honing my skills as a volva had to be my first priority. Danger was coming, I knew it was. I felt it in my bones. I had seen the things that lurked in the wilder magical spaces behind our little township, further north across the lands that I was told ended in Old Norway.

No one ever had gone far enough to be sure, at least not anyone who had come back again to tell the rest of us. But I had been far enough to see the snow-capped peaks of mountains that definitely didn't exist in northern Minnesota. I had even crossed fields dotted with the sorts of rocks left behind by lava flows. The kind you find in Iceland. Which, given that I had walked there and hadn't taken a boat, only made the whole thing more confusing.

Most of Villmark had long ago written off that place as one best left unexplored.

But that was where Loke and Thorbjorn had gone. How far could they have gone by now? Had they reached Old Norway?

Loke had been so cagey about where he thought he was going, I wasn't even sure if that had been his plan. But if it wasn't, why weren't they back yet?

Mjolner brought my mind back to the present with a meow, and I realized I had nearly walked past the street the council hall stood on entirely. I spun on my heel, dodging between farmers with their carts heading uphill to the marketplace until I reached the double doors of the council hall. They were standing open, two young men I recognized from the town patrols flanking those doors. They had weapons on them, but they had more of an air of being an honorary presence than any kind of guard duty.

But I would bet that impression would change in the blink of an eye if anyone inside the hall tried to make a violent kind of trouble.

I gave them each a nod, but I had to pause a moment just inside the doorway for my eyes to adjust to the dim interior. After the bright morning sunshine, even the firelight from the braziers that dotted the longhouse interior seemed dim, leaving the large, windowless space in murky shadow.

"Ingrid!" someone said before I had quite gotten my vision back. But I didn't need to see her to recognize the voice. It was Brigida, one of the council of three. She placed a beringed hand on my arm and guided me across the hall to the steps up onto the platform. "You're just in time, but we have a full crowd today, so please don't feel like I'm rushing you."

"I meant to be earlier," I said apologetically. Now that we were up on the platform, between the largest of the braziers, I could actually see things around me. My eyes went first, as they always did, to the carved pillars that stood behind the three stools where the council members sat. Those pillars had already been old a millennium ago when our ancestors had first arrived on the North Shore. The intricate carvings had once told the story of the founding of their island community back in Norway even further in the past, but those carvings were so worn with time, they were indecipherable now.

Still, I had run my hand over them more than once. Every time I felt a tingle, like I could sense a charge from the weight of time. Like the singing of ancient power. It made me feel connected to all of those people, a chain of lifetimes that had carried on link after link until it had reached me.

But Brigida's hand on my arm was still driving me on across the platform, so I couldn't take even a moment to touch those pillars today. She hurried me past her own stool that stood empty, waiting for her.

Then past the middle stool, which was occupied by Valki, father of Thorbjorn as well as his four brothers. Collectively known as the Thors, they were Villmark's most fierce protectors. So much so that, except on very rare occasions, they were never all in town at the same time. In fact, it was far more common for all five of them to be out patrolling at once, singly or in pairs. But their patrols weren't through the streets of Villmark or the farmlands around it, not like the pair of men I had passed at the doorway. No, their patrols were far out in those wild magic lands filled with ogres and golden-haired temptresses who locked the unwary in their ancient stone towers.

Valki had once been that sort of protector. But when his sons had taken up his mantle, he had settled into his current role of council member and guardian of our ancestral fire. He also directed the street patrols.

Not that he was so old he had to retire from those more active duties, not remotely. To look at him, you'd scarcely guess he was old enough to be father to five full-grown men. And even when he wasn't dressed as he was now in a sleeveless tunic belted over leg-hugging trousers, there was no doubt he was still a strong warrior.

No, I think he'd only done it because he wanted to stay close to his wife, Gunna. Especially now that all of her sons were so often away.

Valki glanced up as Brigida led me by, and as much as he only intended to give me a curt nod of hello, there was always something else there whenever we saw each other. Just a brief expectant flash in his eyes that died the instant our gazes met.

So much information exchanged in that split second of eye contact. Because if he hadn't seen Thorbjorn yet, maybe I had? But if I had, I would look overjoyed even before I could tell him the good news. And I wasn't overjoyed. I was just... waiting. Visibly still waiting. So he didn't even have to ask if I'd heard from his son.

I don't even know if he knew he did that. But it happened. Every time he saw me, it happened.

And my heart broke a little more each time.

My old mentor Haraldr was just settling down onto his own stool as Brigida guided me past it. He needed to use his walking stick for support as he settled onto the low seat, but it looked like he was having a good day. He was dressed more warmly than the rest of us, for sure. But there was so very little fat on his old bones, that was hardly surprising. At least this warm autumn day he felt no need to huddle under layers of shawls and lap blankets to comfortably sit in the drafty, impossible to heat open space of the longhouse.

Still, he was far too old to be sitting on a three-legged stool for hours on end. Not that he would ever listen to any suggestion from me that he should be allowed a more comfortable chair. His house may be a showpiece of modern Scandinavian architecture with its minimalist lines and expansive south-facing windows, but some things still had to be done the old ways. And I knew without asking that his literal seat on the council was one of those things.

"It took a bit of work, finding this stool," Brigida said as she finally came to a stop at the very edge of the platform, just a bit behind where Haraldr sat. "I think your grandmother hid it on purpose. But this was her stool, and her grandmother's before her. It had to be this one."

"Of course," I said, honestly kind of automatically.

But then I saw the stool, and I recognized it at once. I had seen it only one time before. But my grandmother had sat on it in her full volva regalia, sitting in formal judgment over the witch Halldis after she had killed Roarr's girlfriend and attempted to kill me as well.

I had looked for it in my townhouse more than once. That townhouse had been my grandmother's before it was mine, and when I had seen her sitting on this stool, it had been in that living room. But I had never found it.

And never quite gotten brave enough to ask my grandmother about it. She could be touchy about things, especially things related to the house in town. My grandmother had been living in Runde my entire life, only stopping in Villmark for brief visits. I didn't know what about the house she didn't like, but I did know she meant it when she said it was nothing that concerned me.

I could feel Brigida watching me expectantly. I guessed I had stood there staring at that stool for far too long.

"It's perfect," I told her, and mustered up a smile. "Thank you."

"I need to get the meeting started," she said. "This first time, it's okay if you just want to listen and absorb it all. But if you feel compelled to speak up, please do. That's why you're here."

"I probably will just listen," I admitted. Because I had never felt less like any kind of fount of wisdom. Brigida, the youngest of the three, was still more than twice my age. And they had all lived their entire lives inside Villmark. I was still learning how things really worked here in this hidden village outside of the reach of the nonmagical world. And I had found time and time again that just when things started to feel familiar, some new strange custom would spring out at me.

But Brigida was lingering still at my elbow, not moving to start the meeting. And I realized she was waiting for me to sit down first.

I was no fount of wisdom, but I was now an advisor to the council of three. And part of that was keeping up with appearances.

And yet, I felt even less worthy of sitting in my grandmother's place. I knew so little about being a volva still. I mean, I had made a lot of progress in the last year. But all of that had just gone to show me how much longer the journey ahead of me still was.

I wasn't even halfway through the runes yet. I was only up to Iss.

And yet, here I was. Ready or not.

I took a deep breath, then smoothed the back of my tunic over my legs before sitting down on the leather seat of the three-legged stool. The old wood supports creaked a bit, and the leather took a minute to adjust to my backside.

But once I was there, hands resting on my knees with my walking stick on the ground behind me, it felt right.

I might not be ready, but maybe there was no being ready for an office like the one I was taking up. There was just accepting the duty and doing my best.

Brigida must've sensed some of my thoughts, because she lingered for half a second more just to give me the warmest of encouraging smiles.

But then she was gone, crossing the platform to her own stool. As she arranged her skirts around her before sitting down, Valki took the sheathed sword that rested on the ground beside him and used it to tap out a loud, booming call to order on the planks of the platform.

The crowd mingling in the longhouse before us fell into a rustling silence at once. And then our long day began.

CHAPTER FOUR

I GUESS it wasn't exactly surprising that none of the problems that were brought to the council of three by the people of Villmark were anything remotely in my domain. Most problems didn't spawn from magic, and they didn't need magical solutions.

Not that I thought that was all my grandmother had been doing when she had sat in on these meetings. But as much as she looked like a very spry early seventies, she was actually far older. Like, more than a century old. And she had packed a lot of wisdom-gaining experience into those decades. She was very good with people, getting them to work together and not against each other. She didn't need magic for that. In fact, these days she was employing those peacekeeping skills almost entirely in the mundane town of Runde. She had a real talent for both listening to people and, more crucially, guiding them to listen to each other.

I didn't have that skill at all. At least, not yet. I had to cut myself a little bit of a break. I had just graduated from art school when my mother had died and I had moved from St. Paul to the North Shore, to stay with a grandmother I at that time only half remembered.

I had never even had so much as an apartment on my own. I had gone from living at home with my mother to living with my grandmother. I had two places of my own now, sure, but those had both come after I had dipped my toe into the world of being my people's newest volva. I had absolutely zero experience with real "adulting" before I had taken up that very heavy mantle.

And while my magic skills were growing stronger every day, my people skills were still... half-formed. I wasn't *bad* with people. I just was only an averagely competent young woman in her mid-twenties.

There was a reason most people get into political positions when they're at least a decade older.

I knew I wasn't going to be called on to solve any problems, not today. The council would do that.

I was just there to listen and observe. Which sounds easy enough. But that skill my grandmother has at really listening to people? I don't have that. I might have thought I did, but less than an hour into the day's proceedings, I knew I didn't. I could barely focus on the endless complaints of this townsperson or that one.

Even keeping an eye on Skefill and Raggi was less than mind-occupying. Because, as much as they'd pushed so hard to be here, and had earned their seats beside the dais as council advisors, neither of them spoke up. I supposed, like me, they were intending to stick to listening this first session. Surely, eventually, they'd start pressing their particular issues forward. And I expected that pressing to be quite aggressive.

But for now, they just watched and listened.

I really wished I could take out my sketchbook and doodle, but I was very aware that I was sitting up on the platform, where everyone could see me. I had no table to tuck a sketchbook under, no way to make drawing movements look like maybe taking notes or something.

I had to just sit patiently, and try to look more attentive than I was.

But, I mean, the problems were all so very mundane. And it became clear very quickly that most of the complaints were coming from people who showed up every time the council had a petitioning day. Brigida, Valki and Haraldr were good-natured in their ribbing, sure, but it was clear before a lot of people spoke that the three of them already knew what was going to be said.

Take the issue of the apple tree that grew in Geiri's back garden, but half of its branches extended over the fence into Maurr's garden. Apparently, this issue had come up in the past, and the council had agreed that the apples that fell into Maurr's garden were his property. Since Geiri had three other apple trees in his garden, he wasn't out all that many apples. And the tree did grow right on the property line. That judgment sounded like common sense to me.

But now Geiri was back again with a new complaint.

"He's been taking my family's personal cultivar of apples and selling them to my competitor," Geiri said, jabbing an angry finger towards his admittedly smug-looking neighbor.

"I don't brew cider myself," Maurr said, rocking his weight back and forth from toes to heels with an exaggerated nonchalance. "And I can't eat that many apples myself. Not since my wife passed. I don't bake, you see. And that much raw fruit... Well, I'll save you the description of what that does to my digestion."

"Thank you," Brigida said, not quite hiding her smirk.

"I offered to buy every apple, even though they fell from my own tree," Geiri said. "I offered to pay more than they were worth. But still he sold them to my competitor. Deliberately." He said that last word darkly, almost like a threat.

But Maurr just shrugged and carried on rocking and smiling.

"You sold them to Balli? Maker of Balli's Original Superior Cider?" Valki asked.

"I did," Maurr said.

"For less than Geiri was offering you?" Valki went on.

Maurr shrugged again. "I don't think I have to divulge the details of a private exchange. Do I?"

"No," Valki said. "But we all know that means yes. Don't we, Maurr?"

Maurr just shrugged and rocked.

Geiri's face, flushed already, deepened to a shade of red even darker than the apples his family was famous for. But before he could sputter out a word, Valki belayed him with a single raised hand.

"Geiri, we all know that your family's Tiny Orchard Cider is the superior cider," Valki said. "It's the only cider that Ullr serves in his mead hall, and when he's out, most of us get by without it until the next harvest. Because lesser cider just isn't the same."

Brigida looked amused at this tactic, but when Geiri's eyes shot over to her, she just nodded sagely, as if of course she agreed.

"If Maurr wants to make a bad business deal with a lesser brewer, he is quite correct that that is his business," Valki went on. "He's the one missing out both on the coin he could've earned by selling those apples for what they were worth and for not knowing a good cider when he tastes one."

This appeased Geiri, although I could hear him mumbling under his breath that he could just prune back the wayward branches and solve the entire problem that way.

But Maurr's parting words were not under his breath. Although that smile never left his face, he did step closer to the platform to say to Valki, "I see what you did there, so I won't mention any of this to Balli. He might take offense. But given that his cider is the one of choice out at Aldis' mead hall, he wouldn't be the only one. And I see more than a few of her customers in the crowd here today."

He tapped the side of his nose significantly, then turned and walked away before Valki could even start narrowing his eyes at the man.

And just like that, I knew I needed to work harder to pay attention. Because something as commonplace as a dispute between neighbors over apples that fell on both their properties had just unearthed Villmark's deepest conflict of all: that between the isolationists and those who moved freely between our magical world and the greater nonmagical one outside the barrier.

Aldis's clientele were almost entirely the former. And now that Maurr had pointed it out, I did indeed see a few familiar faces in the crowd from my infrequent visits to that hall. Which, given how they all seemed to prefer drinking with their hoods up and their faces in shadow, was really saying something.

Skefill and Raggi had heard those words, of course. And I could see them, speaking to each other in low asides. But they didn't directly address either Maurr or the council.

The rest of the morning was less exciting than the apple tree dispute. There were complaints of dogs barking at night, the derelict status of someone's garden fence, weeds in one person's garden spreading to their fussier neighbor's place.

All things that really felt like the parties involved could come to an understanding on their own, without bringing the council into it. Especially given how readily most of them were to adopt any solution presented to them. The people of Villmark really did just want to get along with each other.

I supposed that came from living not only in a small town, but one that was sealed off from the rest of the world most of the time, and was flanked by dangers on all other sides. They had to rely on each other. They didn't really have any other choice.

We recessed briefly for lunch, but only long enough for the four of us to retreat to the little kitchen in the back of the hall. I had been in this kitchen before. Despite being situated inside of a timber-framed Viking era longhouse, it looked like any other northern Minnesotan kitchen that hadn't been updated since the late sixties or early seventies. There were "modern" appliances, but ones that looked like they might be dangerous to use. And the harvest gold and avocado green color to all of it was a lot.

But we were only back there long enough to pack in the sandwiches that someone had left out on the table for us. We didn't discuss any of the petitions we had heard or speculate on what the afternoon would bring. We just took care of a few necessary activities, then headed back out onto the platform.

Those stools might be traditional, deeply symbolic, and necessary to foster the mood of the brazier-lit scene. But they were far from comfortable.

Well, if Haraldr could handle it without complaining, I could scarcely do any less. But really. Would modern chairs be that much of a change?

Then the petitions continued, and my lunch settled in my stomach in a snug kind of way. The air was warm, and the light from the braziers was so cozily golden. I came to appreciate the uncomfortableness of that stool.

It was the only thing keeping me from nodding off into a nap.

Although it was a close thing, especially as the room grew quieter around us. The petitioners who had already been heard had no reason to stay, so after every decision, fewer and fewer people remained in the hall with the four of us.

But then something changed, something that snapped me fully alert before I even realized what it was.

The other three on the platform had all straightened to full attention at once, I realized, even as I sleepily struggled to do the same. At first I thought someone who commanded attention had entered the hall. But the only people who could do that were the three on the platform with me. That, and my grandmother.

But it didn't take long to scan the crowd of people approaching the platform to be heard. Four men, all of middle age, in the leggings and tunics of the average Villmarker. No sign of my grandmother with her long, thick silver braid down her back.

No sign of Thorbjorn, although I didn't realize until I had come to that conclusion that I had even been hoping it was him. But I was *always* hoping it would be him.

No, it was just four ordinary-looking men. And yet, something about the sight of those men had caught the attention of every member of the council of three.

Not that they seemed nervous or wary. They just sat up straighter, leaned in closer, and looked intent.

Something different was happening, then. Something other than the same complaints from the same handful of people. I glanced across at the faces of the other three for clues, but the only thing I could discern was that they all, for the first time that day, looked genuinely interested to hear what was about to be said next.

Interested, and almost excited. Clearly, they had been struggling with boredom the same as I had all throughout the day. They had just been so much better at hiding it.

But they weren't trying to hide their lack of boredom now. And I found myself matching their body language. Sitting up straighter and leaning in to hear what came next.

What could these four totally ordinary-looking Villmarkers possibly have to say to the council of three that had them all looking so eager?

I was about to find out.

CHAPTER FIVE

"WELL MET, DUFNALL," Valki said to the first of the four men. "Tunni," he nodded to the second, and then, "Litr and Alfvin," to the final two. "The four of you run such a busy business, what matter could possibly bring you before us today?"

Dufnall glanced at Tunni and then Litr briefly before turning his attention back to Valki. "We have run a successful business, Valki. You are quite right about that. We have done very well crafting furniture together, and doing some detailed carpentry work for clients such as yourself and Haraldr here."

Haraldr shifted on his stool to whisper to me, "They installed the bookcases in my library."

"Oh," I said, surprised. "They looked quite old."

"I was one of their first customers, when they were still setting up their own business in the back of Dufnall's father's workshop."

His eyes twinkled at me, but he turned back to the matter at hand before I could respond.

Still, I now had a clear idea of just how good these four men were at what they did. If they had built those bookshelves as one of their first projects together, I knew they must only have gotten better in the years since. I mean, those shelves were overly-stacked with heavy tome after heavy tome. And yet there was not a hint of sagging to any of the shelves. They didn't look like new, surely. But they definitely looked like something well-built, meant to last.

"So why are you here?" Valki asked. "Has someone refused to pay you? Or is someone trying to cheat you on materials?"

The hand resting on his knee curled up into a fist, and I didn't like the odds of anyone who would attempt to cheat these four apparently well-regarded men.

But Dufnall was already shaking his head. "No, Valki. Nothing like that. I guess it's just… the time has come for us to part ways."

"Or so some of us think," Tunni said in a low grumble. His eyes darted off to his left, but whether he was directing that gaze towards Litr or to Alfvin at the very end, I wasn't sure.

"That is a shame," Valki said. "I'm sorry to hear it, of course. But I'm not sure where we three come in?"

Brigida stirred on her stool, and I just caught her shooting a look to the back of the hall, where three women stood together in a hushed cluster, watching the proceedings. They were all in their mid thirties, but beyond that I didn't know who they were. Although something in the way Brigida had looked their way told me she thought the reason the men were here just might lurk among them.

Despite my earlier worries about appearing to daydream and doodle while up on the platform, I found myself pulling my art bag closer and fishing out my sketchbook and then the first pencil to come to hand.

I drew Dufnall first, just a hasty portrait of the three-quarters view of his face that I had from the position of my stool. He had the quiet earnestness that was common both in Villmarkers and in the northern Minnesotans of Runde. He hated being here, I could tell. He didn't like to make a fuss. My pencil found all the little tells of his face, the scrunching of his heavy eyebrows, the tightness around his mouth, all that tension such a contrast to the happily shapeless lump of his nose.

He looked like someone who looked forward year-round to Christmas just so he could dress up like Santa Claus for all the little kids. Not that Villmark had either Christmas or Santa Claus. They had Jule, sure enough, but nothing remotely like Santa Claus.

"The thing is, we always assumed we'd be working together at this thing forever," Dufnall was saying. "The four of us... Well, our business was something bigger than the four of us. We all put everything we had into it."

"And we've gotten plenty back in exchange," Tunni beside him took over. I turned a page in my sketchbook to draw him while he was still speaking. I wasn't particularly trying to channel my magic, but I wasn't *not* trying to either. I wasn't going into my usual fugue state when I drew searching for magical clues to some crime. I was trying to maintain my status as an active listener to these proceedings.

But I also knew that my chance of finding a useful bit of insight from my sketches later was enhanced when the subject was being active, not passive. At the very least, I was far more likely to catch someone in a lie if I drew them while they were actively speaking.

Tunni had the same dark blond to brown hair as the others, the same eyes somewhere between blue-green and gray-blue. And his hands showed the calluses and scars from inevitable minor injuries of his trade. His face was as open as Dufnall's, if not quite as affable.

"We just didn't keep very good records," Litr put in, and I quickly turned another page. Litr was the shortest of the four, although given how tall the average Villmarker was, that was only a matter of comparison. He was nearly six feet tall, I was sure, even if his business partners all had several inches on him. He was also the one of the four who had made the most progress towards the baldness of older age. Even as he talked, the words coming out with a chagrined smile, his hand smoothed down the flyaways that were most of his remaining hair.

"I see," Valki said. "You are needing to split the business four ways. But I'm guessing since you're here now that this is more complicated than merely selling your assets and dividing the proceeds four ways."

"Very much more complicated," Dufnall said. "To begin with, we started out with a lot of help from my late father."

"But that help was never quantified," Litr said.

"And our workshop now is the space I inherited from him when he passed," Dufnall went on.

"So Dufnall should probably get a larger share than a simple fourth," Tunni said.

"But also, we don't want to sell everything and divide a pile of coin," Dufnall said, speaking quickly as if he wanted to get off the topic of his larger share as quickly as possible. He was definitely not someone who ever wanted to be the center of attention. "The three of us, we would like to carry on with the same work, just not together anymore."

"I see," Valki said. "I'm guessing most of the tools and equipment you share through work are from points beyond Runde. Hard to acquire, and perhaps even hard to assign a price to."

"Exactly," Dufnall said.

"And our record-keeping wasn't great," Litr said again.

"That's beside the point," the fourth man finally spoke up. Alfvin. I turned a page and sketched as he spoke. I added a lot of shading, the closest I could get to rendering in black pencil the flushed redness of his face. "What we paid for these things when we acquired them is not the value they have right here and now. They need to be priced again. Fairly."

"No one was ever planning on not treating you fairly, Alfvin," Dufnall said. Although there was a hint of an edge to his usual, affable tone. Impatience, I thought.

Alfvin's face, aside from its ruddiness, was a study in hard lines. The slash of his brows, the jutting angle of his nose. Even his ears seemed to be a hashing of straight lines without a curve among them.

"No, what you were planning was drawing this out over months and months," Alfvin said sourly. I added a few more scowling lines to his brow in my drawing. He didn't strike me as a particularly happy man.

Then I turned another page and drew a sketch of the four of them standing before the platform. It was only as the lines flowing out of my pencil started to gain clarity that I saw something I really should've noticed just with my eyes.

Dufnall was clearly the leader of the four, standing closer to Valki and doing the bulk of the talking.

But Tunni and Litr were both standing closer to him. Closer to Dufnall, but farther from Alfvin. It was subtle. If someone had asked me how they were standing and I hadn't been drawing them, I would've said they were lined up like soldiers, equidistant from each other and from the platform.

But my artist's eye saw the subtleties.

Then I found myself drawing in the clutch of women in the back of the hall. Only three of them. By their ages, I would guess they were the wives of three of these men. So whose wife was missing?

I looked at Brigida again. I had a hunch her little glance earlier had been noting this information. Three wives present and one wife missing. Only, unlike me, Brigida knew every person in Villmark by sight. She knew which one was absent. She had, in fact, specifically noted it.

"This will take time to sort out," Valki said, then lifted a hand to belay Alfvin's objection before he could even make it. "Not months and months, I'm sure. But some time. How much of the equipment in question is from the outside world, just out of curiosity?"

None of the men answered. They just shifted from foot to foot.

"Tunni?" Valki said. At a guess, Valki was poking what he considered to be the weakest link.

Tunni flushed, glancing first at Dufnall and then at Litr. But not answering Valki was clearly a scarier prospect than answering him, although it took him a couple of throat clearings before he could speak up.

"Most of it," he admitted. "At least, most of what's under dispute. The value of the workspace is the other factor. But we each have our own set of Villmarker tools, and no one wants a piece of each other's personal stuff. It's just the larger, modern equipment that can't be divided four ways."

"Plus the workspace," Litr put in again.

"The value of the workspace is a tricky matter," Valki said.

"We have some precedent for it," Brigida put in, and Haraldr nodded.

"We will consider the matter in closed council and present you with our assessment in due time," Valki said. "As to the equipment..."

He trailed off, rubbing his hands up and down the thighs of his leggings. Like whatever he was about to say next, he really didn't want to say at all.

Then, to my surprise, he turned to me. "You have a friend. Down in Runde. He is familiar with equipment such as furniture builders and carpenters use?"

"Andrew is a woodworker, yes," I said.

And he knew about the existence of Villmark. He had even been there once, for Kara Mikkelsen's wedding to Valki's son Thorge. I supposed they must have met there. Because otherwise, I had no idea how Valki knew anything about Andrew at all.

"Would he be willing to assist us in this matter?" Valki asked.

"He would certainly be impartial," Brigida said, amused.

"I can ask him," I said.

"We're going to ask an outsider?" Alfvin asked.

"We're going to ask an outsider to assess your collection of outsider equipment, yes," Valki said drily. "If any of the four of you have any isolationist leanings, I would be deeply amused to hear you defend them now."

The four men all suddenly found the toes of their own shoes deeply interesting. But Raggi and, to a lesser extent, Skefill scowled at Valki's words.

"Very well," Valki said. "I will arrange a meeting between the four of you and Ingrid's Runde friend. The council will meet separately to draw up a plan for compensating Dufnall for his extra contribution to your business. Then we all shall meet to go over our final determination as to how to divide up your business. Is that acceptable?"

Dufnall nodded at once, and Tunni and Litr were quick to follow. Alfvin nodded as well, but grudgingly.

"As a matter of personal interest," Valki said conversationally, "Just why are you breaking up your business? The four of you work so well together. I'm not sure any of you alone is going to match what you did together."

I was pretty sure I caught what he wasn't saying out loud. That Villmark was too small of a community for four separate furniture-building and custom carpentry businesses to thrive at once. From the returning flush to Dufnall's face, I guessed he could hear that subtext too.

"Oh, I guess it was just time," Dufnall said. But as affable as the smile that accompanied those words was, I heard an undercurrent of bitterness in his tone.

I watched him intently, hunting for any clue as to where that bitterness was directed. But he just gave Valki, then Brigida and Haraldr, a nod of thanks before turning on his heel and exiting the hall.

One of the women broke away from the others to hurry after him. The other two women stayed side by side until Tunni and Litr joined them. There was a moment when it seemed like the four of them were going to head out together, but something broke that moment. Tunni and his wife ducked out first, Litr's wife making a big show about searching for something in the basket she had over her arm until Tunni and his wife were far enough away for their paths not to overlap.

That left only Alfvin, still lingering by the platform.

"You have an urgent need for this matter to be settled?" Valki asked him.

Alfvin flushed, but this time in embarrassment, not anger. "I… No. No, it takes as long as it takes."

"And where is Njorun this fine autumn day?" Brigida asked.

"Njorun is at her father's dairy farm south of the town," Alfvin said.

"How are the repairs coming?" Brigida asked.

Many of the farms south of the village had been severely damaged by the hailstorm that had pelted the North Shore two months before. That storm might have been natural, but it had been drawn to and focused on the farms south of the village by magic. Because of Esja, in point of fact, although it hadn't been her fault.

I had visited those farms in the days after, helping to recharge the bind runes painted on the sides of the barns that protected the buildings. I must have visited this Njorun's father's farm at some point, but I had seen so very many farms in such a short period of time that all my memories now were a blur.

Still, I had thought all the repairs had been long-since completed.

But Alfvin wasn't answering Brigida's question. He just lifted his hands as if to show her how empty they were.

Then he slipped them into his pockets and left the hall.

The now blessedly empty hall. Only the four of us on the dais remained. Skefill and Raggi had slipped out after Litr and his wife.

"And you do that every month," I said, getting to my feet to stretch the kinks out of my back. Although most of my aches were in my backside. But there was nothing subtle enough for me to do about it now.

"Only one day a month," Brigida said. "It makes for a long day. But we've found in the past if we have two days a month, they just fill both up with more of the same."

"Having to wait to be heard is a strong incentive to work things out on their own when they can," Valki said.

"Hence the lack of benches," Haraldr stage-whispered to me.

I hadn't even noticed that detail.

But Haraldr's attention had shifted to the sketchbook I had left open on the floor at my feet. He frowned at my drawing of the four men standing before the platform, three of their wives barely sketched into the background.

"You were using your magical sight to glean things we missed?" he asked.

"Kind of," I said. "I don't know the four of them or their wives, although I guess you all do." At their nods, I nodded myself, closing the book to tuck it back away. "I was getting vibes I didn't quite understand."

"Vibes," Valki repeated as if tasting the word.

"And do you understand them now?" Brigida asked.

"No," I admitted. "Is it significant that Alfvin's wife wasn't here?"

"I don't think so," Brigida said, but slowly, as if she wasn't sure.

"Njorun spends a lot of time at her father's farm," Valki said. "It's farther south than Loke and Esja's house. It's about as far south as our community goes. A good distance from any other farms."

"Her whole family prefers to keep to themselves," Brigida said. "As much as she lives in town, she's never really mixed much with anyone here."

"That sounds lonely," I said.

"Well, she goes home to her family quite often," Valki said. "Perhaps she is less lonely there than here."

"Do you think Alfvin wants out of the business just to repair his father-in-law's farm? Or is he intending to move out there with his wife?" I asked.

"Did you see that in your drawing?" Haraldr asked.

"No, not really," I said. "But there must be a reason, right?"

"I'm sure there's a reason," Valki said, clapping me on my shoulder. "But it's not part of what we're called on to deal with. We'll just help them part ways without anger or fighting amongst them. That's our calling. Now, tell me, how soon can you get in touch with your friend?"

"I was heading down to my grandmother's mead hall for dinner," I said. "If I don't run into him there, I'll make a point of going out to find him tomorrow morning."

"Excellent," Valki said.

Then he gave me one last look, one that was filled with a desperate desire to speak about his son. A desire he quashed before it could hurt either of us.

The thing with stillness and waiting is that, at some point, it has to end. Because if it doesn't end, how is it waiting?

The sound from my dream came back for an instant, a rushing sound in my ears like someone was coming up behind me in a pair of skis. But of course when I turned, there was nothing there at all.

And if a person on skis was truly what I was waiting for, how terrible was that?

Because it was October. No one on skis was going to show up for months. And the idea that it might be sooner was too chilling a thought to linger on.

CHAPTER SIX

I

I STOPPED HOME LONG ENOUGH to change into a more Runde-appropriate outfit of jeans and a lightweight sweater with sneakers before heading east of Villmark. I followed the windy trail through the stands of birch trees to the meadow of tall grasses and various wildflowers, all dried now after that early frost, their colors lovely even when muted.

The meadow ended at the edge of the rocky bluffs and the waterfall that fell down to the river that emptied out onto Lake Superior on the far side of Runde. But I didn't make my usual detour to the very edge of the cliff to admire the view and suck in lungfuls of fresh pine-scented lake air. I was in a hurry.

I needed to find Andrew for the council, true enough. But I was mostly anxious just to talk to my grandmother before the crowds arrived at her mead hall hungry for roasted meat and potatoes and thirsty for bottomless mugs of ale as well as her signature honey mead.

So I made a beeline to the rocky outcropping in the center of the meadow which marked the entrance to the cave system that lay hidden beneath the grasses. This was my ancestors' first home in the new world. And it still held special significance to the people of Villmark, although they had all moved into their town a short walk away centuries ago.

The ancestral fire burned here inside a cavern, the fire that had not gone out since Torfa's time. The fire they had carried all the way from Norway. Valki and the Mikkelsen sisters worked rotating shifts guarding those flames, as did Thorbjorn and his brothers, the other Thors. Recently, other volunteers for the Villmark patrol had been added to that rotation. With the Thors so often away from Villmark, it had become too much work for the remaining three.

Although it had been a lot of work for me to convince Valki to accept that help. A lot of work.

I descended the natural stone staircase down to the cavern that was sort of a hub with caves leading out in various directions. I didn't slow my steps as I crossed that room, but I did half-close my eyes, reaching out with my magical senses as I always did when I passed this close to the cave that led down to the prison cells deeper underground.

As much as Villmark only used prison as a last resort to keep the people safe and not as a punishment for crimes alone, there were a few people down there who would never be allowed to leave.

And chief among them was the woman who had tried to kill me shortly after I had arrived in Villmark. The woman who had intended to be my grandmother's protegée before I had displaced her.

Halldis.

She was far weaker now after her long confinement, kept away from anything she could use to feed her own magical power. But she was still as dangerous as ever.

But this day my impressions of her were the same as all the others. Just a soft feeling of malice, too weak to lash out at me, but always aware of my passing.

I headed on to the cavern where the ancestral fire burned hot and bright. Nilda Mikkelsen was there, standing back from the flames and twirling a spear that felt more idle pastime than serious weapons training.

And with her was Esja.

"I thought we were having dinner together," we both said at once. Then traded flushes.

"Kara wasn't feeling well, so I stepped in," Esja said. Then rushed to add, "I left you a note."

"Which I would've seen if I'd stopped in the kitchen, I'm sure," I said apologetically. "I wasn't intending to eat down at the mead hall, but I *did* need to speak to my grandmother. And find Andrew. So I probably should just grab something while I'm down there."

My stomach growled loudly, as if I needed its vote to back me up.

"What about Roarr?" Esja asked.

"I'm sure he'll see your note and work out the rest," I said. "Mjolner stayed behind, anyway."

"Oh, yeah," Esja said. "Mjolner will probably tell him what's going on. Roarr does seem to understand that cat better than I do."

I nodded, not adding that I often thought Roarr understood my cat better than *I* did, too.

"What do you need to find Andrew for?" Nilda asked. And she almost made it sound like a casual question.

But she knew that Andrew and I had been growing pretty close after I'd moved to Runde, before I had officially taken up the role of volva and moved to Villmark full time. We had never actually been dating, but that had been more a matter of lack of time than a lack of interest in each other.

But that moment in time was long gone. I was with Thorbjorn now. Or, I would be. If Thorbjorn were home.

And Andrew was with Jessica Larsen, one of my closest friends in Runde. She ran the café that stood at the crossroads on the highway, a thriving business that kept her busy. But not too busy for dating.

I wasn't jealous of her being with Andrew. But I *was* jealous that they found time for each other. Thorbjorn and I never quite seemed to for more than a few days at a time.

Yeah, I was totally jealous of that.

And I hated myself for feeling that way. Because Andrew had been so sweet about everything, supportive when I couldn't be with him and understanding when our barely real relationship fell apart.

And Jessica was a strong advocate of my floundering illustration career in a way no one else could be. Not even me. I had stopped submitting to book publishers months ago. But Jessica still pestered me for more of my pen and ink drawings to display in her café. I had to keep replacing them because she kept selling them.

She was far better at sales than I was at balancing art and being a volva, that was for sure.

"It's for the council," I said to Nilda. "They need his knowledge of carpentry equipment, actually."

"Interesting," Nilda said, resuming her spear spinning.

"I have a thousand questions about what all that means, but I can tell you're in a hurry to see your grandmother," Esja said.

And she didn't quite hide the shiver that ran up her spine. She was thoroughly intimated by my grandmother. But I couldn't really blame her. When dealing with Esja, my grandmother was in her most cold and remote "wise old volva" mode. I knew it was because she didn't like not knowing exactly what was going on with Esja. But still. I didn't blame Esja for avoiding her as much as she could get away with.

"You're not wrong about that," I said. "I want to catch her before the crowds start pouring in. And it gets dark so early these days."

"Not remotely winter yet," Nilda said as she passed the spinning spear from hand to hand behind her back.

"I know," I sighed.

And with one last wave, I headed on past the boulder that always stood ready to block the way to the final cavern, the open space behind the waterfall itself. The air here was always cool and filled with a fine mist. It coated my skin in chilling droplets, but those soon burned away when I emerged on the far side, back into the warm light from the setting sun.

Although I passed through that all too quickly as I headed down-hill, into the shadow of the ridge behind me. The path was steep enough to require hands as well as feet to get down it safely. But then it leveled out again, winding through a different sort of tall grass than up on the meadow above, more of a wetland grass this close to the winding river.

And then I was stepping out of all that nature, onto the paved patio behind the mead hall. The sun was still setting somewhere behind me, so the building hadn't taken on its guise as a Viking era longhouse yet. The building I walked up to looked like any small town community center with cheap—if recently replaced—aluminum siding and the sort of flat roof that is a pain to keep snow off of. The door I pulled open was a heavy fire door, and the room I stepped into was filled with cheap laminate-topped tables and plastic chairs.

The weirdest thing about that community center which was also a timber-framed longhouse was that neither was properly an illusion. They both actually existed. It was just that they both existed in the same space, overlapping. Some people saw one thing, and some saw the other.

And when the Villmarker crowd with their distinctive Nordic clothing flowed in and mixed with the Runde crowd in jeans, flannel and fleece, no one on either side really noticed the difference. *That* was the real magic of the place. No one noticed anything was weird, except a rare few sensitive types. And they mostly only had strange dreams about it after.

"Mormor?" I called when I failed to find her behind her bar tucked in one corner opposite Runde's combination dry goods store and post office.

"Ingrid," she called back, but from somewhere in the depths of her cellar. She brewed her mead down there, as well as her apple cider. I had been down there before. It wasn't officially off limits to me.

And yet, most times, I just waited at the bar for her to emerge. That cellar felt like her personal space the same way her bedroom in her cabin did. I treated both like a vampire would. I waited for explicit invitations before entering.

Sure enough, my grandmother came up the stairs, her feet in their heavy hiking boots pounding loudly on the old wooden steps. She brushed a stray lock of silver hair back from her face, tucking it randomly into one of the plaits of her long braid, then smiled as she leaned on the far side of the bar from the stool I had slid onto.

"How was your first petitioning day?" she asked.

"Well," I said in a long drawl, by way of preamble.

Then I told her everything, every case and every outcome, from the first to the last. I was aiming for amusing anecdotes, and I earned more than a few quiet chuckles from my grandmother. But still, she seemed strangely subdued.

And when I started telling her about sketching the four men who owned the furniture business together, she interrupted me to ask to see my sketchbook.

I always carried my art bag with me, so I quickly took it out and handed it to her. I continued my story as she examined my drawings. But I started to feel like she wasn't really listening anymore.

"Do you recognize these men?" I asked, not sure why she was studying my sketches so intently.

"Of course," she said. "I know everyone in Villmark, down to little Asbjorn, born just last week."

"Of course you do," I mumbled under my breath. She didn't seem to hear. So I said, "Do you see something I don't in what I drew?"

"Doubtful," she said without a moment's hesitation. "You know, I wished you'd been drawing everyone the entire time."

"Really?" I asked, surprised.

"I know you said you didn't want to look like you were doodling rather than paying attention," she said, which was one of the things I had felt like she hadn't even heard. So I guessed she *had* been listening the entire time. But she went on. "Everyone in Villmark knows you use drawing to access your magic. If you were drawing during council meetings, everyone would assume you were doing that. Not doodling."

"I hadn't thought of that," I admitted.

"I wished you had been drawing Maurr and Geiri," she said.

"Really?" I said again, although with more surprise than before. "You think their argument over the apple tree is important?"

"In and of itself, not really," she said.

"It's because Maurr mentioned the isolationists," I guessed.

"We need to keep an eye on them," she said. But then she shook her head at herself. "No, you do. They never come down here. I can't do much. But you should be watching what they're up to. And casual mentions like what Maurr said, that's going to be where you find your earliest warnings."

"It wasn't much of a threat," I said. "Valki didn't seem worried."

"No, his words were mild," she agreed. But then she tapped her finger on my sketchbook. "That's why you need to be looking for what isn't being said out loud."

I nodded. I could see her point.

She slid the sketchbook back across to me and I put it back in my bag. I couldn't remember if I'd finished the end of my story of my day, but it definitely felt like the moment for that story had passed.

There was something else in the air between my grandmother and me. We both sat quietly for a moment. It wasn't an awkward silence. But it was still a strange one.

"I've been studying the rune Iss," I said. For some reason, my voice was coming out all low. Like I was afraid of being overheard. But there was no one else in the mead hall yet. "And since I've been studying it, I feel like the whole world is holding its breath. Like it's waiting for something."

"Understandable," my grandmother said.

"Because it's Iss?" I asked.

"Well, I was thinking of Thorbjorn and Loke, actually," she said. "The longer they're away, the stronger that feeling of expectancy grows. I assumed you felt it too."

"And Esja," I said. "We all do. Right?"

"Well, there's missing them, and then there's feeling like they were meant to be back by now and aren't," my grandmother said. "I'm not talking about an emotional feeling here. I'm talking about a magical feeling. They should've been back by now."

I swallowed, hard. She was saying things out loud I hadn't even been allowing myself to *think*.

"I've done what divination I know how to do, seeking answers," she said.

"Did you find any?" I asked. But it was a hopeless question. If the answer were any kind of yes, she would've told me already.

So it wasn't surprising when she just shook her head sadly. "Divination is not my forte. At all. You are more gifted in that sort of thing than I am, untrained as you are."

That was news to me. But before I could say anything in response, she was speaking again.

"My skills are low, that's true," she said. "But Loke's energy is strong. Loke is a beacon of magical power even when he's not trying to direct that in any particular direction. Not hearing from Thorbjorn? Well, those men on patrol disappear for months at a time. That's been true my entire lifetime. But Loke? Loke I should sense. Wherever he has gone, he is quite far removed from our world."

"But he'll be back?" I said.

She didn't answer me. But she didn't have to. Not out loud.

Because the sadness in her eyes when they met mine was more than answer enough.

CHAPTER SEVEN

I DIDN'T HAVE long to reflect on that momentary sadness in my grandmother's eyes, though. Because those eyes immediately moved past me to the door behind me, and she shifted all the features of her face into a smile that was almost bright enough to hide the fact that it wasn't in her eyes.

Almost.

"Hello, Michelle and Kristofer. Look who's here!" she said.

And promptly disappeared back down the cellar stairs with the air of someone who needed another moment to pull herself together.

Which, I needed that moment too. But now it was my turn to face the door with as much of a smile as I could muster.

Only in my case, Michelle wasn't fooled for a minute. She crossed the room to pull me into a tight hug and whispered in my ear, "Still no word from him?"

"Not yet," I admitted, my voice hitching a bit. I might have let myself break down a bit more, but Kristofer was standing right at Michelle's elbow. And as much as I liked everything I knew about Kristofer, what I knew about Kristofer didn't add up to much. He was friendly, but a friendly stranger.

And so the smiling mask had to go back into place.

"We came early because your mormor said it was Swedish meatball night. Which is kind of a big deal since you're all technically Norwegian, right?" Michelle said.

"Well, to be fair, Norwegian meatballs are pretty similar," I said. But my stomach growled again at the thought of all that savory meat in cream sauce over mounds of mashed potatoes.

I couldn't smell any hint of anything cooking, though. My grandmother must be cooking up a little magic in the cellar, or she was about to have a lot of angry customers. Because the door behind me kept swinging open and closed as more and more residents of Runde trickled in to find spots at what still looked to them like cheap laminate tables flanked with even cheaper plastic chairs.

"I love meatballs," Kristofer said affably, his hands buried deep in the pockets of his faded blue jeans. "I don't care what country they're from. They're always good."

"Pretty much," I agreed. "There was a restaurant in St. Paul my mother used to take me to that made Yugoslavian meatballs. I loved those. But I don't know how I'd even find the recipe now."

"Tricky," Kristofer agreed.

"Oh," Michelle said, stepping back from me to hurry behind the bar. My grandmother was coming up the stairs with the largest crock-pot I'd ever seen cradled in her arms, and Michelle rushed to take it from her.

"Thank you, dear," my grandmother said. "You can just plug it in at that table against the back wall. There's a power strip there already. And you, young man," she said, turning to Kristofer. "You look like you could help carry a few more of these up the stairs."

"I can, too," I said, stashing my art bag in a nook behind the bar before following Kristofer down the stairs.

There were twelve crock-pots in all, plus equally enormous tureens filled with mountains of freshly mashed potatoes. She had even made my favorite peas, the kind cooked in cream with pearl onions.

We were all going to eat like kings.

The three of us had just finished arranging the last of the crock-pots on the table at the back wall when I was pulled into another tight hug. This one was from Jessica.

"We haven't seen you in an age," she said, glancing over at Andrew as if for confirmation.

"I'm sure Ingrid has been busy," he said diplomatically.

But Jessica, like Michelle, took advantage of the hug to whisper close to my ear. "No Thorbjorn?"

"Not yet," I said.

She tightened her hug briefly, then released me so she could step back and look me over.

"I don't think she's been eating well," she said to Michelle. "Does she look a little thin to you? Thin and pale?"

"I've always been pale," I said. "It tends to come with the red hair."

"There's plenty of food here tonight," Kristofer said. "Let's grab a table so we can make sure she eats."

Then he gave me a conspiratorial wink as Michelle and Jessica debated which table to settle into. Which certainly took the uncomfortable level of attention off me for a minute.

"Andrew," I said, grabbing his elbow and drawing his attention away from the spread of food. "I needed to talk to you for a minute?"

"Sure," he said. A cascade of emotions washed over his face, as careful as he tried to be to hide them all. He wanted to help, but without knowing what I wanted, the question made him a little nervous. Like he was worried I was about to proposition him or something.

"It's about carpentry equipment," I told him.

"That's… unexpected," he said.

I started to explain the situation to him right there by the food table, but we were clearly in the way of the other Runde residents. Michelle and Jessica guided us over to a table even as I continued talking. Then there was a plate of food in front of me, although I wasn't sure who had brought it.

By the time I wrapped up, I knew it was well past sundown. Because, to my eyes, I was now sitting at a table of coarse wood, sitting on an equally wooden bench, and eating my meatballs and potatoes with very solid metal implements from a wooden bowl.

"It's going to take two trips up to Villmark, I think," Andrew said as, finally done talking, I was able to start putting some of that food in my mouth. "One to get a list of the equipment in question, and another to come back with the pricing."

"Is that too much trouble?" I asked around a mouthful of mashed potato.

"Not remotely," he said. "It's just, it used to be a problem for us normies to be inside Villmark."

"They've loosened that up a bit," I said. "At least, the council makes exceptions for my friends. I wouldn't want you to wander alone through the streets on the west side of town, but other than that, it's all fine."

"In that case, let me check my work schedules tomorrow and tell you when I have a spare hour," he said.

Schedules, plural. Because in addition to woodworking, which was really more his occasionally paying hobby, he was also an EMT and helped his grandfather run the auto station kitty-corner across the crossroads from Jessica's café.

"I really appreciate it," I said. "This was the first time I've been invited to join the council while they heard petitions from the people. And it's kind of a big deal, Valki asking me for help. Especially outsider help."

"Well, I'm happy to provide that help," Andrew said.

I spent a very luxurious four or five hours hanging with my old friends, chatting and laughing, eating even more meatballs before dancing myself to complete exhaustion.

And then I climbed back up that steep hill, through the caves, and back across the meadow and birch trees to my house in Villmark. Other Villmarkers were making the same hike with me. A few of the drunker ones were singing some song together. Nothing I knew. Although their words were so garbled, I wasn't even sure which language they were singing in.

Spirits were still high, and the night was deliciously warm.

Mjolner was waiting for me on the front porch with all the palpable impatience of any teenager's parent when they're out after curfew.

"They would've loved to see you," I said to him as I let myself in the front door.

His yellow-green eyes just blinked at me slowly, unimpressed with my lack of an excuse for being out so late.

But he had completely forgiven me by the time I was cleaned up and in my pajamas, climbing into bed. He let me settle in first, then promptly curled up with his spine pressed against the back of my neck.

I fell asleep to the lulling vibrations of his purring.

I didn't focus before drifting off on any sort of magical work. I didn't even give the rune Iss a single thought. My ears were still thrumming from the music back in the mead hall, and I was simply too exhausted to try to use my dreaming time productively.

Still, even without trying to, Iss was in my dreams. Or, at least, the shush of skis over snow was.

I couldn't say for sure, but it felt like those skis were drawing closer. Always unseen behind me, and still off in a distance.

But closer. Ever so slightly closer to me.

CHAPTER EIGHT

I woke the next morning to find myself absolutely freezing. For half a second, I thought this was a lingering impression from the dream of the approaching skier. I can dream quite intensely, even when my dreams aren't magical in the slightest. That's been true since I was a very little kid. It fueled a lot of my early artwork, my extensive memories of my dream world.

But I opened my eyes to see my breath fogging in the air, and I knew this was no hangover from my dream. The temperature had really plummeted overnight. Which isn't unthinkable for northern Minnesota in the autumn. But this was a little extreme. I would almost swear I could hear the crackle of frost when I threw back my blankets.

I just had time to register that Mjolner was gone from my pillow—and must've left some time ago since there was no lingering indentation from his body there—before I raced across the room to dig through my drawers for my warmest sweatpants, an oversized cardigan with a shawl collar, and thick wool socks. I even pulled a beanie down over my unbrushed curls.

Then I went down the stairs to look out the floor to ceiling windows that graced the south-viewing wall of my living room. I could look out over two-thirds of Villmark from there, as well as the hills beyond.

Or, at least, normally I could see those things. This particular morning, all I could see past the frost that coated the glass in a sparkling sheen was a dense gray fog. Not even the fence between my garden and that of my closest neighbor's was visible.

I took a moment to turn on the geothermal heat pump for my radiant in-floor heating, then decided to head outside and take a look around. I laced up my warmest hiking boots and pulled my parka on over my bulky sweater. I was sure I looked like a polar explorer as I headed out my front door, but as cold as it was in my sealed-up house, how much colder must it be outside?

I stepped outside, and the intense chill of the air froze my first breath inside of my lungs. My eyes teared, then those tears promptly froze to my lashes.

Quite a bit colder, then.

I zipped the collar of my parka up to my nose and fished my heavy gloves out of the pockets just where I had left them at the end of the last winter. Even with all that, the tops of my cheeks felt a sting I knew all too well.

It was cold enough for frostbite to be a real hazard. Even though it was still mid October.

There had been nothing in the weather forecast remotely like this.

No, I was pretty sure something magical was going on. I just had to figure out what, exactly, that was.

I pulled up the hood of my parka until it covered those cheeks, then took my first steps out into the fog.

I could hear people doing the same in the fenced-in gardens around me, their voices muffled and echoing eerily through the mist. It was like those voices were drawing closer, then farther away, then closer again, but never getting close enough for the words to become clear. I couldn't even tell whose voices I was hearing.

Seeing anything was completely out of the question, too. The fog wasn't just a cloud; it was filled with sparkles of dull light. Sometimes they looked like drops of water reflecting some unseen light source, but mostly they looked like dancing flakes of snow that never quite reached the ground.

The ground that was snapping icily under my boots as I walked. Like all the bricks of my front patio had been glazed over in a thin sheen of ice.

I had just reached my front gate and was fumbling with the latch with my bulky gloves when I saw a flash of a different sort of light reflecting off of the dull metal of that latch. The fog was making everything either dark gray or cold silver, but the flash of light that caught my eye was warmer, more golden. Like sunlight, although the sun was still an hour away from rising, and that would be directly ahead of me, not behind me.

No, this was more the glow of firelight.

I turned, but saw nothing behind me. I was only a dozen steps away from my front door, but the entirety of my house was already lost from view.

Although I got the sense that it was there in the fog, looming like a dark obstruction between me and what I was looking for.

I walked back the way I had come, my boots crunching over ice coating the same patio tiles all over again. Like it had reformed entirely just in those few seconds since I had stepped on it last.

But I didn't go back inside. No, I circled around to the corner of my front garden that led to the narrow path that led between the south wall of my house and the fence beside it. The path that led to my back garden.

I had never spent much time in the back garden. Someone— perhaps my grandmother or perhaps even her mother—had once grown herbs there, and from time to time I had the urge to clean the space up, to clear out the weeds and let the herbs that still struggled to live there flourish once more.

But there were always too many other things I needed to do. It had remained an unfulfilled urge for a year now.

No, I never used it. But since she had moved in, Esja had taken over that space as her own. Not that she was inclined to gardening either. But she entertained her guests there, I'm sure because of the practically assured privacy since *I* never went back there.

She also used it as her weapons training space.

What we never used it for was cooking or any kind of fire. I had a small grill that saw some occasional use, but it was in the front garden. And there was no fire pit in the back. Just the overgrown beds of herbs and a small square of lawn that was more creeping Charlie than proper grass.

And yet as I approached the back corner of my house, when that garden should be coming into full view if not for the fog, the sparkles that swirled lazily in the fog before me definitely had a golden glow to them. Like they were reflecting firelight, firelight that was coming from that patch of lawn.

The sounds of flames crackling over wet logs reached my ears, distorted by the acoustics of the fog but distinct all the same.

Then I reached the edge of that lawn and finally saw the fire itself. It was a roaring bonfire, flames dancing over a stack of wood that must stand chest-high on me. Only when I saw it did the smell hit me, the thick smell of wood burning when it was still too green.

I buried my nose a little deeper inside the collar of my parka and pressed on. Because I was pretty sure I could see something in the fog between me and that fire. There was a flicker of a shadow, a wisp of something there. But like the snowflakes, it kept lazily dancing about, refusing to be pinned down. Refusing to take a proper identifiable shape.

Another voice reached my ears then, a deeper voice I knew at once. Even through the echoes of the fog, the words were distinct. The only problem was, they were in a language I didn't speak.

But it was one I recognized. And the minute I knew what I was hearing—the old tongue that predated Villmarker Norse and probably Old Norse as well, the tongue that Esja spoke in when she was channeling gods or spirits or whatever was actually happening to her—I lunged forward.

Because that wisp of a shadow swaying before me was *way* too close to that fire. And that fire was roaring hotter than ever.

I could feel that heat all over my body, burning the fronts of my thighs even through the thickness of my sweatpants. Making me break out into a sweat under my heavy winter layers. But still the wisp refused to take form.

I tore off my gloves and reached out with my bare hands and only a vague desire for magic to work through me. I wasn't forming thoughts well enough to do any actual magical work.

But it didn't matter. That little bit was enough. Whether it was that flare of magical will or just the touch of my bare skin, this time when I reached out I caught hold of an elbow.

And then, it was like that touch brought her into full shape. Esja, standing barefoot on the icy ground, the diaphanous folds of her sleeveless nightgown flapping around her as if she stood in a high wind. Although, inside of that fog, there wasn't even enough of a stirring to the air to explain the dancing of the snowflakes.

"Esja?" I said.

But her eyes when she turned them to me were completely whited over. Whatever was speaking through her mouth, it wasn't Esja. Not now.

She said something to me, something in such a haughty tone that it was probably just as well I couldn't understand a word of it. Then she twisted her arm, a subtle little motion that happened faster than I could even see. It broke my hold on her, leaving my formerly grasping fingers stinging a little.

I heard another voice calling through the fog, although the words were unclear. It felt like the sounds I couldn't quite discern were probably someone's name. Someone lost in the fog, maybe close by, but maybe on the far side of the village.

But I couldn't focus on it to learn more, because Esja was spinning away from me, spinning in a sort of dance all around that bonfire.

It was a crazed dance. I tried to keep up with it. Not even the intense light from the bonfire was breaking far through this fog. Even halfway around that fire, Esja would be lost to my sight.

But she just spun faster and faster, her bare feet as nimble as any ice skates over the slick ground beneath us. The fire didn't seem to be melting any of that frost. It was just tempering it into a hard glaze.

Then the inevitable happened. Esja's dance carried her too close to those roaring flames. And the flapping edges of her thin nightgown caught fire.

It was happening again. Esja was on fire, for the third time in as many months.

And, to my horror, all I could do was stare at her.

CHAPTER NINE

I

The fog thickened around me, like it was holding me back, constricting me like Jack in a giant's hand.

Then a bit of the fog rushed past me. A wave of gray with no sparkling snow within it. Just a smothering roll of dark gray advancing like a storm front, if oh so much faster.

It brushed past me, and I felt a scratching like coarse wool over the back of my bare hand. Then that brushing became more of a barreling as something impacted my shoulder. I didn't slip, but I was staggered enough to where I had to throw my arms out to keep my balance.

I was out of the giant's grip now, anyway. I could move again.

Not that I needed to. Because what I had taken to be just another part of the fog turned out to be Roarr, still in his pajamas although with his feet in hiking socks, the gray kind that were red at the toe and again at the heel. It was a weird thing to fixate on, I know. But he already had Esja in his arms, the flames that had been licking all around her smothered by the folds of that fire blanket.

Where had he even gotten a fire blanket?

But even as my mind formed that question, I already knew the answer. From Andrew. As an EMT, he would know where to acquire such things, and which ones were the top-rated.

I didn't even have to ask why he'd gotten a hold of one. After Esja had caught fire twice before, it was a sensible precaution.

Although I did wonder why he hadn't told me about it. Or why he hadn't left it stored somewhere I could've gotten to it if I needed to.

Not that I had been any help in this instance. All I could do was blink stupidly at the two of them, whispering together as one asked and the other confirmed that Esja was, indeed, all right. And quite herself once more, if a bit shaken up.

Then the stupid just kind of cleared out of my mind. Like the sun dispelling a fog. Something really had been holding me back. Maybe not a literal giant's hand closed around me, but something in my mind had kept me trapped there, unable to help Esja.

But Roarr had gotten through just fine. Either that was very lucky for all of us, or whatever had trapped me had allowed Roarr to move freely. For some unknowable reason.

I didn't like that train of thought. I was much happier when I was trusting Roarr.

"I'm okay," Esja said, to Roarr, but more loudly than before. "Really. My nightgown is mostly gone, but I have others. I don't think my skin was touched at all."

"It wasn't before," I said.

"Is this going to keep happening to me?" Esja asked.

"No," Roarr said before I could so much as open my mouth. "No, that was the last time."

I bit my lip, but didn't contradict him. As much as I felt in my gut that Esja was working her way through the Norns and now, after this last fire, had finished with the last of them... well, it was just a theory.

But what good would it do to say so out loud? It would just make Esja anxious, and for no reason. Whatever was going to happen was going to happen. She was as powerless to change that as I was.

Which was a terrible feeling. One I would spare her, if I could. For as long as I could.

"I saw the fire from my bedroom window," Roarr said, still hugging Esja tightly. Although, given he was wearing no more than his pajamas, this was as likely as much for his comfort as for hers. I could see him shivering, although she seemed quite snug inside the folds of all that wool.

I, on the other hand, had torn off my gloves less than half a minute before. And already there was no sign of them through the thick fog. I put my hands deep into the pockets of my parka and walked around half-hunched over, retracing my steps and searching every inch of the ground for a hint of those gloves.

But the fire that had been raging so tall was guttering out now. Not surprising, given how green that wood was and how wet the conditions were. But without its light, I didn't like my odds at finding my gloves again.

I'd have to go inside for another pair.

Which was fine, because my two roommates both needed to get warmer clothes on themselves.

"Come on," I said, abandoning my search to herd them back towards the front door. "You two grab some hot showers and warm clothes. I started up the heat pump, but it's going to take a minute for the interior of the house to get comfortable. In the meantime, I'll make some coffee."

"Thank you," Esja said. Her tone was thick, and her raised eyebrows made sure I caught her real meaning. As much as I knew she appreciated my plan for the morning, I knew that wasn't what she was thanking me for.

She was thanking me for not grilling her about what had just happened, what she remembered, what she had done before things had started getting crazy.

I gave her a nod of acknowledgement, but it was a little insincere of me. Because I knew as soon as she was settled in, warmer and calmer than she was now, I was totally going to start hitting her with all those questions.

Not that I thought the answers would help. But still. I had to ask. It was my job.

No, more than that. It was my nature.

The drone of voices lost in the fog had never entirely gone away. As long as I had been outside, I had heard hints of others in Villmark moving around, talking to each other, trying to figure this strange weather out. But as we passed into the front garden, I realized that at least a sizable percentage of the voices I was hearing were standing outside my own front gate. Debating, apparently, which of them should knock.

"We'll get dressed," Roarr said. Leaving unsaid what all three of us knew: the rest of our plans were about to be thoroughly dashed.

Which was a shame. I really needed that coffee.

But I just nodded my thanks as the two of them hustled their steps over the icy ground and inside the house.

I buried my hands deeper inside my pockets, as if I could grasp handfuls of the warmth their fleece lining provided.

Then I opened the gate latch. The metal was cold, the kind of cold that sucked warningly at bare flesh. It wasn't quite like when I was a kid and I put my tongue on the monkey bars at the playground, but it was pretty close. The minute the latch was open, I pulled my hand back with a hiss and thrust it back into its pocket, where it throbbed at me angrily.

"Ingrid?" someone said, as if they weren't sure it was me. Which, given the fog, was a fair question. It would be all too easy to knock on the wrong gate in this weather. And I couldn't see any of the faces gathered around me. I just had a vague sense of darker gray shapes against the backdrop of lighter gray. Their edges were indistinct, as if they were far away. It was only by the size of them that I knew they were actually standing quite close to me.

"Well met," I said. "Strange weather we're having."

"Indeed," someone else said. They were both men, and they sounded familiar, but not anyone I knew well. Perhaps men on the patrols, or men on the farms to the south. People I would nod to as we passed on the street.

"Apologies, Ingrid Torfudottir, but I don't think you grasp the full extent of it."

That voice I *did* know. It was Skefill. I could even pick out the outline of his shadow from the others. He wasn't taller, exactly. But he stood taller, if that makes any sense. Even enveloped in fog as he was, he still *loomed*.

But hearing his voice, the vague impressions I had of the others solidified in my mind.

"You're all on patrol?" I said. Only kind of a question.

"Indeed," said the same man who had offered that single word before.

"We have something you need to see," Skefill said, and he took a step closer. Not that this was enough to bring him into clear view. But it did add to the looming feeling. Although I wasn't sure he was doing that on purpose.

At least, not this time.

"Me, not Valki?" I asked. Because Valki was the one in charge of the patrols. As much as there had always been friction between him and the isolationists—well, between him and anyone on the patrols who wasn't one of his sons—there was a chain of command that everyone had agreed to respect.

After that one time when some of them hadn't. Not that Skefill wanted to be reminded of that now.

But I could see the outline of his shadow shaking his head. If he knew what I had just been thinking, he didn't show any umbrage at it. He just said, "No, this is definitely something *you* need to see."

"It's volva business?" I asked, and just managed not to say those words with a sigh.

"It's most definitely volva business," he said.

Then the "indeed" fellow finally said something else.

He said, "The entire village is encased in a wall of ice. And there's no way out. Not over, not under, and definitely not through."

I wished I could see any of their eyes. Because what I was really wishing was that they were all having a joke at my expense.

But I couldn't see their eyes. And I didn't even need to, to confirm they weren't joking. They might not be right about how dire the circumstance was, but they weren't joking about what they thought they had seen.

I could tell now, from the energy in the shifting of their feet and the way their shadows seemed to be glancing at each other. They felt trapped. They truly felt like we were are all trapped. The entire village. All trapped.

Together.

Considering how many of Skefill's friends—as well as Skefill himself—lived outside of the limits of the village, I knew none of them would joke about this, ever. Not even at my expense.

"I need to get some gloves," I told them. And probably a scarf, and my winter hiking pants. But they didn't need a full list. "I'll just be a minute. Do you want to come in while you wait? I have coffee."

"No, we'll wait here," Skefill said.

"Do you think something is inside the village?" I asked him. I tried to pitch my voice low, so my words were only for him. But with the weird fog acoustics, I doubted anyone gathered around me failed to catch my words. Or the edge of fear even I could hear in my wavering tone.

Great. This volva was really inspiring confidence this morning, that was for sure.

But Skefill was shaking his head again. "No, not inside."

He spoke those words so darkly, their second meaning was clear. But I just nodded, then sprinted back to my house to grab what I needed and add more layers to what I was wearing as quickly as I could.

Not inside, he had said.

But what he had meant was, outside. Something was outside. And I didn't think the ice wall that had sprung up out of nowhere was some kindly divine gesture of protection.

No, we were in danger. All of Villmark. Again.

And with Thorbjorn gone and my grandmother down in Runde, I was the one who was going to have to step up and protect everyone.

Preferably without getting frostbite.

CHAPTER TEN

THE GOOD NEWS WAS, when the sun finally rose high enough in the sky to reach the streets of Villmark, it made short work of cooking off that snowy fog. The air was still bone-chillingly cold, but it was possible to see now. And, without a single cloud in that cold blue sky, the sun provided a lot of light to see by.

But the bad news was, Skefill and his patrol weren't wrong about that ice wall. It was too tall and too slick to climb over. The ground beneath it was frozen too solid to tunnel under. And it was far too thick to attempt busting out of it.

Skefill and his team had been patrolling since midnight, so as soon as they had shown me that wall at the point where it crossed the road between the last of the houses of Villmark and the sod-roofed structure of Alldis' mead hall, I sent them to find beds where they could. Every one of them was now effectively homeless until this wall was dealt with, and I had no idea how long that was going to take.

Unless we had the most epic of all Indian summers, I didn't see this much ice melting until March or even April. The angle of the sun was too low in the sky and the days were already too short for it to make a dent in that deeply blue glacier.

"How does this even happen?" Roarr asked once he, Esja, and I were alone with the wall. He pressed one gloved hand against the ice, then leaned close until his nose was nearly pressed against it.

It was like staring down into the ocean in a way. Just blue and blue all the way into depths where nothing more could be discerned. I couldn't even make a guess as to how thick this structure actually was. But it was thick. It was really, really thick.

"Magic," Esja told him with just a hint of a teasing smile. She, of the three of us, seemed most comfortable in the sudden cold. I mean, her cheeks had dots of deep red on them, as did the very tip of her nose. But her scarf hung loosely around her neck, and I had to remind her twice not to touch things without her gloves on.

Even with the sun up, frostbite was still a real danger. And one that could strike quicker than you'd expect.

"It goes all the way around the village?" Roarr said.

"We should walk the perimeter, just to be sure," Esja said eagerly.

I just shrugged. It was as good of a first step as any. And it had the added advantage of putting me in a position where a lot of Vill-markers would see me. They would know I was working on the problem.

Although I was sure Valki and maybe even Brigida would track me down and pepper me with questions I couldn't answer soon enough.

Yes, definitely being on the move was the better plan.

It was slow going, walking around the entire village. Because everyone else was curious about the wall as well. We were constantly encountering groups of people attempting to climb over the wall or break through it or even tunnel under it. But all of them were coming to the same conclusion as Skefill and his patrol had.

While it only seemed to be about thirty feet tall, and while Vill-mark had plenty of rope on hand, no one had managed to get a grappling hook to stay lodged safely on the top of the wall to climb up. And the surface was too slick for free climbing, although plenty of people were trying.

Some were even trying it with their gloves off. And so far all they had to show for it was the first signs of frostbite in whitish-gray patches on their skin.

No one could hammer a single stake into that wall either. It was impenetrable, even to the sharpest of stakes or the strongest of blows.

Ditto trying to break through it. Axes, hammers, even chainsaws just bounced off the surface with nary a scratch left behind.

Tunneling under it was the method of escape that was abandoned the quickest. The deepest, darkest, coldest days of January didn't see ground as hard as the ground under that ice wall. Trying to dig down into that was too demoralizing for anyone to make much of a go at it. Although I few did indeed try, if only long enough to know how hopeless it truly was.

Aside from the many people attempting to break out of Villmark, others stood around in groups talking quietly with each other. It was like no one, despite the bitter cold, was staying inside today. I paused to mingle with as many of those clusters of people as I could, always asking questions.

No one had seen the wall form. No one had heard a thing. No one had even noticed the fog. It was like we had all been placed under a spell, a magical sleep that kept us inert until this cold work was done. Then we all woke at once, confused, blinded by the fog. And completely trapped.

By noon, we had made a complete circuit of that wall. It was intact everywhere, never getting any shorter or any taller, and presumably never getting any thicker or thinner.

It also stood apart from the last house on every road, far enough back that even getting up onto the roofs of those homes didn't offer a view past that wall. I could, at one point, just glimpse the top of the trees on the tallest hill to the west, but that was all. Nothing closer.

And as for my cellphone, I had no signal at all. I couldn't even make a 911 call, let alone send a text to my grandmother.

Which didn't worry me a ton, actually. Because if she didn't know about this wall already, she would soon enough. No one coming out of Villmark was something she was bound to notice. And then she'd investigate.

Although I did regret we couldn't put our heads together on this one. I relied on her as my sounding board. Each of us working the problem separately might lead to a solution eventually, but it would happen so much faster if we could just communicate with each other.

"No one is panicking," Esja noted as we finally left the enigma of the ice wall behind and headed home to make something warm and filling for lunch. I was pretty sure I had some leftover potato soup in the back of my freezer. That with the last of the bread in the breadbox would be perfection.

"I noticed that too," Roarr said. "Is it just because they're too shocked to panic yet?"

"Panic might still be in the future, but I don't think that's why no one is panicking now," I said. "Or maybe it's just me, but this wall doesn't exactly feel like an evil thing, does it?"

"It avoided all the houses," Esja said. "It's not a perfect circle because of it. Maybe that's not significant. I have no idea if perfect circles of ice are more work or less than imperfect ones. But I keep thinking of that house in the far southwest corner of town. Do you know the one I mean?"

"The one where the ice sort of formed an extra alcove, like it was skirting around the rabbit hutches?" Roarr asked.

"Exactly," Esja said, smiling up at him. "Like whatever made that wall, it didn't want to get too close to those rabbits. And they were cold, I'm sure, before the family brought them inside. But if the wall had gone where it looked like it was supposed to, they'd have been buried in the ice."

I hadn't noticed any of this at all. But I had been talking to the mother of that particular family. She had been struggling with insomnia for months, but last night she had gotten the deepest, most refreshing sleep of her life. Even waking up before dawn as we all had hadn't spoiled it for her.

"Interesting," I said. "Walls are often protective. Maybe that's what this is."

"Well, then I know when panic is going to set in," Esja said, still half grinning. "When people start asking each other what they think this wall is protecting us *from*."

"I don't want to contemplate it," Roarr agreed.

I thought she had far too much of a point to find the humor in the situation myself, but I decided not to call them out on it. It was called gallows humor for a reason.

And it was often a human necessity for a reason, too. Panic wasn't good for people. Humor lets you keep terror at arm's length.

For a time, anyway.

"I have to come back out after lunch," I said. "I need to draw. As much as I can in this cold, anyway. I get the same protective vibes as you two do, but I still don't like it."

"It feels like a parent overdoing it," Roarr said. "We're not children. We can protect ourselves."

"Maybe," Esja said with a tip of her head that was almost like a shrug. "Maybe not. But I'd still rather know what's out there. And when it's coming. And who did all this," she finished, lifting her hands into the air. We had left the ice wall out of sight behind us, and we couldn't see it down any of the smaller roads we were crossing on our way home. But she managed to encapsulate the entire situation with that little gesture.

"I'll draw after lunch, but I have a different mission for you two," I said.

"Anything," they both said, as if with one voice. They exchanged a glance, but didn't quite burst out laughing.

"I need someone to compile a list of who's inside the wall, and who's outside of it. Most people were probably sleeping in their own beds last night, so I don't expect too many surprises. But I want to know who's missing, and who's… extra."

"Sure," Roarr said. "I can check with the patrols. Some of them probably already know that information for their routes."

"Good call," I said. "Esja, I want you to track down Valki if you can. It's weird that he hasn't found me yet."

"We've been walking all day," Esja pointed out, but I was already shaking my head.

"He can always find me when he needs me. The fact that he didn't yet today might mean nothing. But just in case, I want you to check in with him."

"Sure thing," she said. "Maybe he's setting up extra patrols again. Like last month, when that thing was hunting us in our own streets."

"Maybe," I said, but I didn't think so. "But one thing I want you to ask him in particular." And it was something that was really going to come better from Esja than it would from me.

"What's that?" she asked.

"I need to know which Thors are inside this wall," I said.

I tried to make that sound casual. Not remotely like this was deeply vital information.

But I didn't fool her for a minute. She just looked at me, her cornflower blue eyes assessing me shrewdly.

"Ingrid," she said, startled enough to stop walking even though we were still half a block away from my front gate. "You think the answer is zero."

"I don't know," I said, although that was, in fact, my current greatest fear. "I don't know, but I *want* to. So that's why you're going to go ask."

Because if I asked myself, that little awkward moment that always passed between Valki and me the instant we were in the same room together might escalate into a full-blown mutual panic attack.

But coming from Esja? Coming from Esja, it was hopefully just a question, one with no particular baggage attached to it.

Although maybe that wasn't going to work. Because he would know Esja was only asking because *I* wanted to know. Still, I had to know.

Because if the answer really was zero, I was going to have to put some real effort into not being the first person in Villmark to start panicking.

CHAPTER ELEVEN

I

DRAWING outdoors in the winter is never my favorite thing. Because there's really no way for me to do it with gloves on. No matter how thin the material, it's always too awkward. The pencil slips in my hand. I can't use the side of my hand to blend properly. I lose enough sensation that I tear the pages sometimes.

And yet it was so cold that even if I were wearing those thin gloves, my hands would be freezing.

The best I could do was draw in short bursts with lots of hand-warming breaks. Which wasn't great for getting into a flow state. And yet, I couldn't think of a worse idea than getting into my full-on flow state. My fugue state. I lost track of everything when I was in that head space. Time, the world around me, my own body. Nothing existed except what I was creating between the pencil and the paper.

That was a recipe for frostbite, for sure.

So I made do with the short bursts of drawing. But I wasn't exactly surprised when nothing emerged from those drawings. There were hints of things in the shadows deep within the ice, but nothing I could identify at all. They weren't runes. They weren't even properly shapes. But there was something there.

Esja caught up with me by midafternoon, bringing with her a very welcome thermos of hot tea. I took a break from drawing to wrap my hands around the warm exterior of my mug and put my cold nose into the steam that was rising from its surface.

"Thorge is here, and so is Thoralv," she told me, and my body all but sagged in relief. "They've been trying to break through the wall with hammers and log splitters and the augers they use for ice fishing, but so far, no luck."

"Let me guess, not even a scratch?" I said.

"I saw it myself," Esja said. "They were going at it with everything they had. And yeah, not making the slightest mark on the surface. I don't think this is normal ice. I mean, who knows how thick it is, but aside from that, we should still be able to chip it. If it were normal ice, we would."

"Well, given how it showed up overnight while the entire town was in what must have been a magical sleep, it stands to reason it's not normal ice," I agreed.

"Do you see anything in your drawings?" she asked.

"No," I said between sips of tea. The warmth felt so good in my stomach. "I'm having trouble with the cold, though. I'm not sure there's a way around that."

"I was thinking—" Esja started to say, but then her eyes darted to something past me. "Wait. Here comes Roarr."

I turned to see Roarr walking briskly up the road towards us. Was that about using the exercise to keep his body warm, or was there some urgency driving him on?

But when he lifted his hooded head to give me a nod of greeting, I was sure it was the former. I was just so on edge; I was seeing danger everywhere.

"The census is underway," he said. "It's going to take some time to get a full count, but so far, no one has been reported missing. There were people out on the farms or hunting in the west who aren't currently in town, but not anyone who should've been here at the time."

"That's something," I said.

"How's the drawing going?" he asked.

I felt a surge of annoyance that everyone was asking me that question. But it made total sense why they would. So I swallowed down my first impulse to say something snappish and just sighed. "Not great."

"Yeah, too cold, right?" he said. Then he went on. "I was talking to Skefill. His sister's house is very near the edge of town, you know. The wall is totally visible from their upstairs windows. And they have a couple of dormers in the attic they've converted to a children's playroom with a really nice view. I don't know how close you have to be to do what you do, but maybe a higher angle would help? I mean, in addition to being inside where it's warm."

"Roarr, I could kiss you," I said.

Roarr's cheeks were already red from the cold, but they flushed even more deeply. Esja laughed and gave him a punch in his arm, one I'm sure he could barely feel through all of his layers of clothing. But he rubbed the spot with one mittened hand, anyway.

"She's still grateful for what you did for her before," he told me.

"What we all did," I amended. "I didn't save her on my own. You both helped. And her brother and the patrols as well."

"Sure, but she's grateful to *you*," he stressed.

"Well, I'm not achieving anything here, so I might as well take her up on her offer," I said. I only had a couple of hours of daylight left. Although since she lived on the west side of town, the windows she was offering that overlooked the wall would be west-facing too. That would give me a little bit more time, anyway.

"I passed Thorge and Thoralv on my way here," Roarr said as I packed up my sketchbook and pencil, fumbling with the flap of my bag with my gloved—but still sightly numb from the cold—hands.

"They're still at it?" Esja asked. She sounded impressed.

"Barely," Roarr said. "Not even chainsaws were making a dent. I'm not sure why they thought their muscles and a hammer were going to do more."

"Hubris," Esja said with a shrug. Her blue eyes were dancing.

It was nice that no one was panicking, but how long could that go on? When would people start feeling trapped? In a day? Or two?

Certainly not longer than that. As much as we were used to long, hard winters where going outdoors was a huge undertaking, this was more than that.

Then I had a sudden thought. "Does anyone in town have explosives? Like for stump removal or anything?" I asked.

Esja lifted her eyebrows at me in quiet surprise.

But Roarr mulled over my question carefully. "Maybe," he allowed at length. "I think that would be more common further out, in the farms and houses outside the ice wall. But I can certainly check around."

"It's entirely possible that the people on the outside are trying to get in at the same time we're trying to get out, right?" Esja said.

"I certainly hope so," I said, thinking of my grandmother.

"Nilda and Kara are outside of the ice wall," Esja said. "They were guarding the ancestral fire together. They must've noticed when neither Valki nor I showed up to relieve them this morning."

"Of course they were on duty," I said, just fighting the urge to slap my own forehead. "No wonder Thorge is destroying his body trying to bust through the wall. His wife is on the other side."

"It's a shame your phone doesn't work," Esja said. "Otherwise we could have one of your friends in Runde go to Kara and let the two of them talk to each other with your phone."

"Yeah," I said. But mostly I was thinking, it had only been a day. They had been apart longer than that before, when Thorge was on patrol. They would be apart longer than that again in the future, many, many times.

And I forced myself not to think of how much longer it had been since I had seen Thorbjorn last.

"Valki had a few other messages for me to deliver to other people, so I should hop to it," Esja said. She was trying to sound put upon, but she wasn't fooling me. After a long childhood of being a sickly invalid, being called on to do important work was still a real thrill for her.

"Of course," I said. "We can catch up at dinner."

"I'll walk you to Skefill's sister's house," Roarr announced. Not that

I needed an escort. But there was something in the tone of his voice that just had me nodding my agreement.

The three of us walked together for a couple of blocks, but then Esja parted ways from us with a wave, jogging downhill to the south end of town.

"You had something you wanted to say," I guessed the minute Roarr and I were alone. "Something you didn't want to say in front of Esja. I'm guessing it's about what happened this morning?"

"You were there before I was," he said. "I saw her from my bedroom window, just like I said. But I didn't see you down there."

"It was less than a minute," I said. "From when I reached her to when you came out of the fog with that fire blanket."

Given how long it must've taken for him to run down the stairs, then around the house, likely I hadn't even been there when he'd been looking out the window.

"I saw her standing before the fire with her arms up like she was pulling something down from out of the sky," he said. "It was too much like that first time, when she had… what did you call it? Channeled chaos?"

"I don't think that's what was happening this time," I said.

"Okay," he said, but not like he really believed me. "When I got down there, she was already on fire. By the time I got the flames out, she was herself again. I didn't see that not-thing in her at all. But I wasn't looking until after I'd put the flames out. Did I miss anything?"

"Well, I can't see what you see," I said. "She did the thing she had done on the longship last month. Where her eyes go all white and she speaks in that older language? But it was only for an instant."

"So she was still herself when you got there?" Roarr asked.

I stopped walking and really thought about what I had seen. "No," I had to admit. "I don't know if she was. Maybe?" But I played it back in my head again. "I heard her talking before I saw her. And she was talking in that other voice."

"So not for an instant, then," Roarr said. "Maybe a lot more than an instant."

"I don't know where the wood came from," I admitted. "I don't keep firewood back there. I don't even have any sizable trees. Just a few shrubs behind the herb beds. It was green wood, too fresh for burning, really. But did she chop down a neighbor's tree just to build that fire?"

"I didn't see anything out there last night," Roarr said. "Not that I was looking specifically. But I'd think when I was looking out my window yesterday, I would've noticed a pile of wood that isn't usually there."

"I believe you would," I agreed. Roarr was generally pretty observant of details. And given how close an eye he kept on Esja when she was in that back garden, either training or entertaining guests, I had a hunch he looked out that window more often than he'd want to admit.

"So did she go into that white-eyed state first, then cut down a tree and build that fire?" he asked.

"I suppose that's more plausible than what I was assuming," I said.

"What's that?" he asked, cocking an eyebrow at me in curiosity.

I felt my cheeks flush but said the words anyway. "That the bonfire just kind of appeared? Like the ice wall?"

"Do you think the two are related?" Roarr asked.

"Well, I didn't before," I said, perhaps a tad too aggressively.

"Two odd, magical things happening together in one night? Isn't that a lot of coincidence?"

"Esja also set herself on fire last month, remember?" I said. "That turned out not to be remotely connected to that thing coming out of the lake to hunt our streets. *That* was just a coincidence."

"Okay," Roarr said with a slow drawl.

But I knew what he was thinking. "Right," I said. "Two coincidences in as many months do feel a little too coincidental."

"And yet, without more clues as to what's going on, who knows?" Roarr gave in with a shrug.

We had reached Skefill's sister's house, but he lingered at the edge of the cobblestoned road rather than following me up the front walk.

"You have another job to get to?" I asked.

"Well, it's not like I can help you draw," he said with a dry laugh.

But then he grew serious again. "Some of the people who live closer to the wall, they think it's closing in around us."

"What?" I asked, shocked at the idea. I wasn't claustrophobic, but the idea of being trapped in ice was still not a pleasant one.

"I'm not sure it's true," he said. "It might just be people getting nervy. It's not weird for some of us to start feeling like we're trapped, right?"

"I'm surprised it's not happening with more of us yet," I admitted.

"Right," he agreed with a nod. "Which is why I'm going to set up some markers to measure where the wall is now."

"That's not a bad idea," I agreed.

"Yeah. I was thinking at the end of the main roads. That covers north, south, east and west. A decent sample size. I'll set markers exactly one meter in from the wall, and measure them again tomorrow to see if there's any change."

"That's an excellent idea, Roarr," I said. "If the wall's closing in, we'll know. And if it's not, we'll be able to prove to people that it isn't. Truly, good thinking, Roarr."

He flushed at the compliment, but just mutely nodded at me. Then he lifted one mittened hand in farewell and headed north to get started.

He really was doing the work to regain the trust of the Villmarker community. I had to commend him for that.

And Esja was working just as hard to gain everyone's respect as a member of that community. I knew how much that meant to her, to have value in the eyes of others.

Roarr wasn't wrong. I hadn't really thought through how long Esja had been in her altered state before she had caught fire.

But I wasn't sure he was right to think the ice wall and her bonfire were connected. The ice wall had already been there when I found her, for one. Fully formed while we all slept.

Or, at least, all save Esja. She didn't remember being awake, but she must have been. She had built that fire. That would've taken time. Time that must have overlapped with the formation of the ice wall.

But if she had been doing all that magical work from my own back garden, I would've known. I would've sensed it. Maybe not when I was in the grips of the magical sleep—and didn't I hate the idea that I was as susceptible to that as everyone else in town?—but when I was standing there behind her while she danced around the bonfire. I would've felt it then. Even if her spell had been done by that point, the lingering traces of such potent magic would've been screaming for my attention.

No, I didn't think she had formed that wall.

But the idea that the wall had been formed to contain her, or whatever the thing working through her had been doing?

That fear was going to be a lot harder to shake.

CHAPTER TWELVE

A LONG AFTERNOON spent sitting on the hard, bare wood floor of Skefill's sister's attic with my sketchbook on my knees had resulted in dozens of drawings. But the only real takeaway for those hours was a very sore bottom when I finally gave it up and struggled back onto my feet.

I hadn't once gotten into a proper fugue state. I had slipped into my artistic flow state a few times, but as pleasant as that always was—to get swept up into the motion of my pencil over the paper and the sound of graphite scraping on the fine grain—it wasn't helpful as far as figuring out what was going on was concerned.

Roarr and Esja were cooking together in the kitchen when I got home. I set my things in my art nook, then made a quick pass through the living room, then upstairs to my bedroom.

There was no sign of Mjolner. I hadn't been home all day, though. And I could scarcely blame him for not finding me himself today, given how bitterly cold the temperature was persisting in being. Still, I did wonder what he was up to.

I knew he could travel anywhere he wanted to, pretty much in the blink of an eye. He could move through walls, although I had never quite seen him do this. He was secretive. Which was probably just a cat thing.

But I wished I knew one thing for certain: whether he had disappeared from my pillow before or after the wall had gone up.

Because if he had left Villmark for whatever reason before the wall came up, was there something about that wall that was trapping him outside of it now?

I didn't like that thought at all. I spoke of a power greater even than what I already knew we were up against. So far, that wall still felt protective in my mind. But if it was keeping my cat from me? That started to feel a touch more sinister.

I was still lost in my own thoughts throughout dinner. I could tell that Roarr and Esja both noticed, but their exchanged glances made it clear they intended to let me stew without interruption.

I'm sure they thought I was doing something productive inside my own mind, when all that was really happening was that the same questions were spinning around and around. Without some new input, I could never find any answers.

Before heading upstairs for the night, I paused at the floor-to-ceiling windows to look out over the south end of Villmark. The wall wasn't quite visible anywhere in my view, but given that it was a partly cloudy and totally moonless night, I couldn't see much anyway. Just my breath fogging the glass when I stood too close.

After getting ready for bed, I did take a minute with the sketchbook I kept on my nightstand. I hoped to get my mind in an open state for dreaming about the rune Iss, but just drawing straight lines over and over felt too much like a sketching warmup. And I had already done so much drawing that day. I finally gave it up entirely, switching off the light and curling up under the weight of my heaviest duvet.

And missing the warmth and the purrs of my cat. It took longer to fall asleep when he wasn't there to soothe me.

Then I woke, far too soon, to a pounding at my front door.

That was never a good sign.

I threw back the covers, shoving my feet into slippers and grabbing my hoodie before heading down the stairs.

Roarr was already at the door, speaking with someone out of sight in the predawn darkness. I heard footsteps behind me and knew without looking that Esja was also up. Up and, knowing her, dressed and alert. I rubbed tiredly at the tangled mass of my hair, then stepped up behind Roarr.

It was Skefill again, with the men of his patrol standing behind him, barely inside my front gate. The air outside was still breath-stealingly cold, but at least there was no fog this time. I could see them well enough in the light from the streetlamp behind them.

"What's going on?" I asked, tucking my hands into the sleeves of my hoodie and crossing my arms to keep warm as I joined Roarr in the doorway.

"Again, there is something you should see," Skefill told me.

"Let me grab my coat," I said, and turned to find Esja already thrusting it out towards me. She had her own parka on already, her feet in boots and ready to go.

"Me, too," Roarr said, and Esja stepped outside to speak to Skefill, leaving the mudroom space for Roarr and me.

"Something with the wall?" I said to Roarr as I struggled with the laces of my boots.

"He was vague, but that was what I gathered," Roarr said. "He said it's on the west side of town, just south of the marketplace."

"What's there?" I asked with a frown. I was too tired to summon a mental map myself.

"It's just south of my parents' house," he told me. "Nothing but more residences. I guess we'll find out when we get there."

I only remembered I had left my art bag in my nook after I'd finally gotten my boots on, and was just kicking myself for that when I saw it waiting for me on the step that led up to the rest of the house. Esja must've snatched it up in passing when she'd followed me down the stairs.

At least one of us was thinking clearly. Although the minute I stepped outside and got my first lung-full of bitter cold air, my brain snapped into sudden clarity. Extreme cold is better than a caffeine hit, if nowhere near as pleasant.

"Do I get a hint as to what this is about?" I asked Skefill even as I struggled to keep up with his fast pace over the icy cobblestones.

"It could be an accident. It could be foul play," he said. "I'd prefer for you to draw your own conclusions when you see it."

"Okay," I said with a yawn. "But we're definitely talking about a dead body, then?"

"A man, yes," Skefill said. "I can't see his face well enough to tell who he is. Or, rather, was."

"You can't see his face?" I repeated, not liking the sound of that at all. How violent was this death? And yet, apparently Skefill felt like "accident" was still on the table. So what did that mean?

But Skefill was just shaking his head. "This is why I wanted you to see it first. We should walk faster."

Because falling on my butt on a frozen cobblestoned road was going to make everything so much better. Still, I did try to move faster.

We followed the main road that my town house was on south for two blocks past the marketplace, still closed up for the night, the wider street eerily quiet under the light from the LED lamps. Then we turned west and walked past residence after residence. Everything looked perfectly normal for a predawn morning, every house quiet as the family within slept.

"He's in the middle of the road," Skefill said, pointing with his chin as I saw the wall ahead of us. The cobblestones ended at the last pair of houses, but the road continued on past it. Well, it was more well-defined dirt path than proper road, but that path was going in the same direction towards the hills to the west of Villmark.

"I don't see a body," I said to Skefill as my gaze swept over the ground between us and the wall of ice twice. But even in the dim light of the moonless night, I should be able to make out the darker outline of a body on the lighter gray of the road.

"He's there," Skefill said, pointing.

"In the middle of the road, you said," I said, still not seeing what he was pointing to.

"In the middle of the road, but also inside that wall," he said.

Then he led me up to the wall itself, and I finally saw what he had been pointing at. A man, stripped to his underthings, sitting up but slightly slumped over his own knees, like he was taking an exhausted rest.

But he was entirely inside the wall of ice.

"That wasn't here yesterday," I said. Because I had walked the entire perimeter in good light. I would've noticed a man trapped inside.

"No, he wasn't even here earlier this evening," Skefill said.

"Then it's true," Roarr said. "The wall is closing in. This man sat with his back against it and got swallowed up."

That certainly looked like what had happened to him. But I had so many more questions. Like why hadn't he felt the ice closing in around him and moved away? Why was he all but naked in this killer cold?

Why was the surface of the ice as flawlessly smooth and straight as ever? That wasn't, in my experience, how ice formed. At least, not vertically like this. Like a skating rink set at a 90-degree angle.

"I should check my markers," Roarr said.

"Go," I told him without looking away from the man inside the ice. Skefill was right. With his head bowed down like that, it was impossible to see his face.

But, was this murder? It looked like he had just sat down to rest for a moment with his back to the wall, and then had become part of the wall.

And yet…

"Why is he undressed?" Esja asked. "And where are the rest of his clothes? I don't see them in there or out here anywhere."

"I can't tell if he's been tied up in any way," Skefill said. "Perhaps when the sun is up, we can see better."

"When the sun is up, we have to figure out a way to get him out of there," I said.

Although I didn't like the odds on that. Nothing anyone had tried the day before had made so much as a scratch on the surface of that ice. Until I figured how to break the spell creating the ice, I was afraid this guy would be trapped just as he was.

"Valki took a census yesterday," I said to Skefill. "We can take another one today and find out who's missing. That should tell us who this guy is."

Middle-aged, I could see. Long hair in a shade between dark blond and light brown. Average height for Villmark. Average build. No sign of any tattoos or scars, but through the ice, that kind of detail was really hard to see.

He could be anyone.

"Some of the guys on my patrol wanted to start knocking on doors in the area," Skefill said. Then he gave me a steady look. "I wanted to bring you in first."

"Thanks for that," I said, sincerely. But I had to sigh. "I'm not sure what good I am, but I appreciate the gesture."

"We can't get to him," Skefill said.

"No, I don't think so," I agreed. "Maybe it was just a tragic accident? There's something called paradoxical undressing. When someone has hypothermia, they can feel like they're actually too warm and they'll start taking all their clothes off. It was certainly cold enough last night for hypothermia."

"I have heard of such things happening," Skefill said with a nod. "But only in remote places. Far to the north or west on hunts. Out on the ice of a lake when fishing. Usually someone caught out in a storm, unable to find their way back to shelter. But this?" He lifted his hands, gesturing to the many sleeping homes all around us. "Why was he wandering the streets so far past the point of feeling symptoms?"

"At a guess, he was out drinking?" Esja said. "I still wonder where he left his clothes, though."

"*I* wonder who took his clothes from him and forced him to sit against the wall until he became one with it," Skefill said.

"I understand why you're thinking along those lines, but maybe don't speak such theories aloud?" I said to him. "We don't want people to think we have another supernatural predator stalking our streets. Especially not now, when we're effectively trapped here."

"And if we do have another predator?" Skefill pressed.

I chewed my lip, uncertain how to answer that.

"He looks so peaceful," Esja said, cupping her hands around the sides of her face as she gazed into the ice. I had a wild urge to pull her away like a child from a stove. The ice had swallowed up that man, and there was no hint now if that had been a fast or a slow process.

At the very least, her nose must be absolutely freezing.

But she stepped back on her own, a wistful sadness on her face. "It's like he's napping. Like if we could just melt this ice, he would wake up again."

"He will not," Skefill said with firm certainty. Then he took a half a step closer to Esja, like he wanted to lend her some comfort after the harshness of his words. But he was all too aware of my disapproving presence so close beside him. So he just gave her arm a squeeze with his mittened hand. A squeeze that lingered just a hair too long.

"Roarr set up markers all around the wall yesterday," I said. "First thing to know is if the wall is growing everywhere evenly, or if something unique happened right here."

"It'll be dawn before he makes it back to us, then," Skefill said.

"We can't remove his body, but we should do something to cover him. Shouldn't we? I mean, he's basically naked," Esja said.

"There are tarps in the storeroom behind the council hall," Skefill said. "For when we set up tents and canopies in the commons on special occasions. We can set up a tent large enough to cover the end of the road, but leave the fourth wall tied up so that anyone who needs to could still see inside the ice."

"Excellent plan," I said. We would be securing the crime scene, basically.

"I'll send two men to do that for you," Skefill said.

"What are you going to do?" Esja asked.

"The rest of us will walk the perimeter," he said.

Then he gave me a nod before gathering his patrol together to issue commands. But I caught his meaning well enough. I knew what he had left unsaid.

He was going to walk the perimeter, because he needed to be sure in his own mind that only one Villmarker had been swallowed up by the wall. Because one might be murder or might be a tragic accident.

But more than one? That was a real problem.

And I had dreamed nothing useful the night before. I still had no clue how to get rid of this wall around us.

And the fact that it was closing in quickly enough to swallow an entire person definitely added a ticking clock to the whole problem. I needed to figure out what was causing all this, fast.

Before more people got hurt.

CHAPTER THIRTEEN

THE TWO MEN Skefill had left in charge of setting up the tent weren't anyone I knew. I suspected by their quiet attitudes and their wardrobe choices that steered more towards furs and wool than space-age fabrics that they were isolationists.

But for once, that didn't matter. They worked together quickly and efficiently. By the time the approaching sunrise started lighting up the sky to the east, the tent was up. It sat against the ice wall, spanning from one side of the road to the other. Esja checked from both sides on the outside of the tent, but from either vantage point, it was impossible to see the man trapped inside.

People would wonder about the tent, but with so many different tests being conducted on the wall, it wouldn't be seen as particularly suspicious. Or so I hoped. Once Valki and Brigida were awake, they'd surely march down here at once to see everything for themselves. That would prompt some questions.

Esja appointed herself as guard of sorts, standing outside the flaps of the tent with her swords clearly visible, even if her usual leather armor was not because of her parka.

Then Skefill's two men returned, this time with a brazier from the council hall as well as my own stool from the dais.

"What's this?" I asked as the man with the brazier set it in the center of the inside of the tent and got it lit.

"For light and warmth," he said. His words were even, but his face was bemused. Like mine had been the strangest question he had ever heard.

"For while you draw," the other man said, setting my stool close to the fire from the brazier.

"Oh. Of course. Thank you," I said.

They just nodded, then departed. For a moment, when the tent flaps were open as they passed through, I heard voices from outside. Some of the closest neighbors had come out to see what was going on. Esja was talking to them, explaining how I was doing volva things and couldn't be disturbed by anyone save the council.

Which was a nice cover story. I wished I had thought of it myself.

But Skefill's men weren't wrong. I really should be drawing the man inside the ice.

I sat down on my stool, finding it no more comfortable for drawing than it had been for listening to petitions. But the fire was warm enough to let me take off my gloves for minutes at a time, and the light penetrated into the ice without merely reflecting off the surface with dazzling brightness. Which was a big help.

I drew every detail I could see of the man from the curve of his thumb as he semi-clasped his own shin to the lock of hair that had remained tucked behind one ear.

Something was familiar about that lock of hair, although the more I thought about it, the less I felt like my brain could finish making the connection. So, being as Zen as I could, I stopped trying to think and remember and just focused on the drawing.

"You drew him before."

I jumped at the voice so close behind me. I had never heard the tent flaps moving, felt the rush of cold air as someone passed inside, noticed the bright light of the morning sun that briefly eclipsed the softer light from the brazier. But I was no longer alone. Brigida was there, standing behind me and bending over my shoulder to examine my drawing with a studious frown. So all of those other things must have happened too.

"You recognize him?" I asked.

She didn't answer at once, just stepped around me to approach the wall of ice. She studied the man trapped inside there for several minutes before turning back to me.

"Yes, but I have the benefit of already knowing who it must be," she said. "He was reported missing, and everyone else in Villmark is accounted for."

"Who is it?" I asked. Because if I had drawn him before, I must know him. And yet I was still drawing a blank.

"That is Dufnall," she said.

It took me a moment to place that name. "He is one of the four carpenters who are dissolving their business, right?" I said.

"Yes," she said. "He's a quiet man. A family man. He and Ronnok have four children, all under the age of ten."

"A quiet family man," I said, touching the lines of the drawing on the pad before me, as if that somehow held a connection to the man himself. "What you're saying is, you don't think he got drunk, stripped off his clothes, and collapsed in the road by the wall, then?"

"I would find that scenario highly unlikely," she agreed.

"Bad blood in business," I said. "Always a popular motive in murder."

"Valki and I thought much the same," she said. "We've already checked in with Tunni and Litr."

"And?" I said.

"They and their wives are all alive and well," she said. "They also have alibis for the night, although those alibis were staying home with their wives and children. So."

"Do you have reason to doubt their word?" I asked.

"No," she said with a sigh. "That's where you come in. You are much better at asking those sorts of questions and getting answers than Valki and I are."

She nodded her head towards my sketchbook in case I had missed her meaning.

It sounded like I was going to have another full day. But this would be a full day of questioning people about Dufnall's death. Which was important.

But it would be a full day not spent figuring out anything useful about the wall.

Then another thought struck me. "Wait, you mentioned Tunni and Litr, but not Alfvin. Isn't Alfvin the one who wanted to dissolve the business in the first place?"

"I'm not sure if he started it. He was certainly the most keen on making sure he got his equitable share, and quickly," she said. "But with the damage to his father-in-law's farm, that's understandable, too."

"You don't think he did this, then," I said. I knew I sounded skeptical. Or puzzled, anyway. It was a big conclusion to leap to so early in our investigation. Unless she knew Alfvin better than I had thought.

"Oh, I know he didn't," she said. "He's not in Villmark, currently."

"He isn't?" I asked.

"No. When we took the census yesterday, he and his wife, Njorun, were both among the number of people who were outside of the area when the wall appeared. Presumably at her parents' farm."

"But no one knows that for sure?" I asked.

"Their neighbors speculated," Brigida said. "But that speculation was based on the two of them spending more and more time on the farm. So."

"Sure," I said. "And anyway, this still might not be murder. This could still be a crazy, random accident."

"I almost hope that ends up being the case," Brigida said.

"Almost?"

"Usually, anything is better than murder, right?" she said.

"But not this time?" I asked.

"People are starting to talk," she said. "And, to be clear, very few people know what happened to Dufnall. Still, I'm hearing things."

"What kinds of things?" I asked.

"People say the wall has been… singing," she said.

"Singing," I repeated dully. "I think I would've heard that."

"Not everyone hears it," she said. "But that's how it goes in some of the old stories, right? Things lure you away from safety through music only you hear. Alvs do it, in some stories. Sirens or harpies. I've even heard tales where people hear singing in celebration out in the woods, and when they go to investigate, all they find is the Wild Hunt."

"Sometimes stories are just stories," I said. "I mean, that last one doesn't even really make any sense. If they find the Wild Hunt, they don't come back. So who knew they were hearing music?"

"Someone who failed to keep them safely indoors," Brigida said with a shrug.

"I never heard any music," I said. And I had definitely been as close to the Wild Hunt as anyone could get and still make it back alive. I knew what I was talking about.

But Brigida just tipped her head to one side, as if conceding my small point but not the larger ones.

"You think the wall lured Dufnall into stripping off his clothes and sitting against it until it swallowed him whole?" I asked.

"I think it's a magic wall of impenetrable ice that appeared overnight and is closing in around us," she said. "I think the stories are going to continue to spread. Whether or not they turn out to be true, the fear in people's minds is already real. And it's going to grow."

"Unless we stop it," I said.

"I will do what I can, of course," Brigida said. "I've already been spending my days talking to as many people as I can. Yesterday was easy. There was some trepidation, but no real fear. Today is harder. Tomorrow? Well, if word gets out about Dufnall, tomorrow may prove a real challenge to my powers of keeping people calm."

"I suppose in this case, murder would be the preferred thing to be dealing with," I sighed. Because murder everyone understood. It was tragic, dying because of a fight over the distribution of goods from a business. But it wasn't the kind of tragedy that might visit you and yours next. Not if you trusted your business partners.

"I don't want a scapegoat," Brigida said. "I do want a thorough investigation into the truth of the matter. And as much as I trust everyone I spoke to, I know you see things I do not. I would take it as a personal favor if you would speak to the widow as well as the other two families inside Villmark."

"Of course I will," I said.

"I do realize this keeps you from dealing with the problem of the wall itself," she said.

I summoned up a shrug. "I wasn't making any progress on that, anyway. Perhaps a break to focus on something else will let me come back to it with fresh insight."

Which sounded nice. It almost sounded like it could be true.

But the thought that kept coming back to me all through the morning, as I talked with Skefill and as I drew what I could see of Dufnall, was that I couldn't remember a single thing I had dreamed the night before.

Had there been the approaching sound of skis again? I didn't think there had been.

But why was that lack now feeling so significant? I didn't even know what it meant. Or if it was related to the wall at all.

Still, I found myself eager to get through the day, just so I could get back to bed and sleep again. To see if the dream recurred.

I missed the sound of those skis.

CHAPTER FOURTEEN

I EMERGED from the tent to find Esja there, just as I had expected her to be. But standing with her was Roarr. The two of them were speaking intently, faces close together. I could only see the back of Roarr's head, but the look on Esja's face as she listened to him was grave.

"Trouble?" I asked.

Roarr turned to look at me. But then his eyes roved around, taking in all the people who were loitering around the tent, not even pretending to have any reason to be there besides curiosity.

"It's just a test, my friends," Brigida said to the crowd as she emerged from the tent behind me. "We're trying some techniques for breaching the ice that work better without sunlight interference."

I couldn't even imagine what those "techniques" might be, but no one in the crowd called her out on that. Although one woman piped up to ask, "Any luck?"

"Nothing so far, but it's a slow process," Brigida said with a bright smile. "We do have our keenest minds brainstorming possible solutions inside the council hall. Have any of you been?"

There was a murmur of voices from the crowd, but mostly shaking of heads.

"Everyone is invited to contribute," Brigida said even as she started east down the road, back towards the center of town and presumably then south to the council hall. "We have hot sandwiches for all, and Ullr brought in several kegs of his finest ale. Which may not have the reputation for great inspiration that Nora's mead does, but it will certainly keep you feeling warm inside."

This prompted a few chuckles that mostly sounded like polite noise to me. But as she continued walking, a good percentage of the crowd peeled off to follow her.

And most of the rest of the crowd dispersed on its own. Although two tall men remained, standing uncomfortably close to where I was still hoping to speak to Roarr and Esja.

"It's all right," Esja told me. "Brigida brought these two members of the patrol to guard the tent so I can stay with you today."

"That was thoughtful of her," I said. I tried to give her a quizzical look, one I hoped conveyed the question, "Do they know what's *inside* the tent?"

But I wasn't sure if she caught it. She just touched one and then the other of the guards on the arm, whispering a few last-minute instructions to them. They nodded and stood up a little straighter, shooting warning glances at the few neighbors who were still standing out in the cold in the vicinity of the tent.

"You don't have to drive them off," Esja assured them. "Just, no one gets inside save the council or Ingrid."

They both thumped their fists on their chests as if taking a silent vow, and Esja took me by the arm to guide me back up the road.

"Do you know where we're going?" I asked her. Because that was one piece of information I had completely neglected to get out of Brigida before she had left.

"I know," Roarr said. "Dufnall's house is just north of the market-place. We'll turn here and cross the market road on the west end, and then it's just another couple of blocks."

"Is the marketplace even open for business?" I asked. Because, gawkers aside, very few people seemed to be out in the streets of Vill-mark on this cold but sunny day.

"The central area where the bakeries and food shops are is open," Esja told me. "The shops on the west end, the blacksmith and the artisan shops and, of course, the furniture-making business, are all closed for the time being."

"Most of the people attempting to break through the wall are either part of the idea-gathering meeting in the council hall, or are making attempts at the very south end of the circle," Roarr told me.

"Why there?" I asked. "Does it seem thinner there or something?"

"Fewer houses," Esja said.

"Yes, with the gardens jutting so far south of the rest of the village, the wall swung out wide of most of the houses. There's more space there to work without disturbing anyone's home," Roarr said.

"Okay," I said. "I was afraid people would think it would be easier to break through there because it's further south. And it's really not that much further south."

"I'm not saying *no one* thinks that," Roarr said. "But mostly it's the space thing."

We reached the marketplace, and while there were people visible to the east of us, they were several blocks away. No one was around to hear us talking at this end of the street.

"So what were you two whispering about when I came out of the tent?" I asked.

"Just the results of my measurements with the markers," Roarr said.

"And what were they?" I asked. "I assume the circle really is closing in on us. But is it the same everywhere?"

"So far, yes," he said. "We lost nearly a meter last night. I set up new markers for tonight."

"He wants to know if we lose a meter every night, or if it goes faster or slower," Esja said.

"I'll track it every night, just to see if there's a pattern," he said. "I would expect it to advance something more than a meter tonight. And more than that tomorrow."

"You think it's going to speed up?" I asked.

"Not exactly," he said. "It's just, every time it advanced in towards the center, it's a smaller area that it's trying to cover. A smaller circle."

"Oh, sure. Hit me with geometry on top of everything else," I said. But really I was pleased. If he was willing to tackle the math for me and give me real answers about what was going on, I had to appreciate it. I could do math just fine. I had held a straight B in all my academic classes all through high school and art school.

But I didn't *like* math.

"He has a notebook," Esja whispered to me, but not in a way that made any real attempt for Roarr not to hear. "Very meticulous records of numbers. Although he tells me he can't start making real charts to track rates of change until he has more data."

"Well, it's true," Roarr said. But his cheeks were flushing in that not-from-the-cold way again.

"I didn't exactly meet Dufnall and his wife..." I trailed off, uncertain.

"Ronnok," Roarr said.

'Thank you. I didn't meet Dufnall and Ronnok properly when they petitioned the council, but I know them on sight," I said as we crossed another east-west road and I knew we had to be drawing close to our destination. "I gather since he's about forty, but all of his kids are less than ten that neither of you know him at all?"

Including Esja in that was just to not make her feel excluded. I knew she had spent nearly all of her days inside the confines of her family home until very recently. And as much as she had met many young men since moving into town, I didn't think she'd made the same kind of inroads with happily married couples.

"I only know him to nod to," Roarr said. "I'm not sure I've ever even seen his wife." Then he tipped his head and said, "This is it."

He and Esja fell back to let me climb the steps to the front door first. But I had only just lifted my hand to knock when the door swung open, and I recognized Ronnok standing there looking out at the three of us.

She looked like she'd aged a decade in the few days since I had seen her last. Her eyes were red, if currently dry, and her hair had been pulled and tied back from her face without the benefit of brushing it first. She was wearing the typical Villmarker woman's clothing of an apron dress over a woolen sheath dress, and yet the dark orange color of the apron dress clashed aggressively with the yellowish-green of her sheath dress. Like she had grabbed half from two different matched sets to create a whole that was not complementary at all.

I wondered if she had noticed and decided she didn't care. Or if she just wasn't seeing color at the moment. I had days, shortly after my mother had died just when I was about to graduate from art school, where either of those things could've been true. I remembered that feeling of protective detachment well.

"Brigida told me to expect you," she said as she stepped back to let us all in.

"We're so sorry for your loss," I said before I let myself step inside.

"Thank you," she said, but like it was merely an automatic response. "I'm not sure what I can tell you that will do any good at all. But I promised Brigida I would talk to you. So. Here we are."

"Yes," I said, slipping out of my boots and hanging my coat on one of the hooks by the door.

"The others are on their way. I expect them any moment," she said. I could hear how numb she felt in her voice. She was barely holding it together.

I really wished I didn't need to bother her with questions now. But I had to. Maybe the presence of the others would help.

"You're close? With..." I wracked my brain for the names of the other women.

"With Oda and Arnóra, and even with Njorun, although we don't see her as often as we'd like," Ronnok said. "We've all been close since we were toddlers, really. We were all born in the same month of the same year. None of us are even cousins, but we've always felt like sisters."

That was a relief. If anyone needed a couple of sisters here with her now, it was Ronnok. She looked like she was wavering on her feet.

But then she gave herself a little shake and stood up straighter. "I've made coffee," she said, then hurried out of the hallway in a way that told me she absolutely needed a minute to get herself together before we followed her.

Not that I had to do anything to delay the others. There was only room by the door for one of us to get our boots off at a time. And Roarr was so tall that sitting on the bench there didn't leave enough space for getting around his own knees to get to his boots.

And they had four young kids in this snug little house. Dufnall had been the one who started the business with the workshop space his father loaned to them all, and then later his father's entire workshop when he passed.

But a quick poke of my head into the living room before following the others into the kitchen showed very worn furniture. The couch had been covered in a knit blanket, carefully tucked in around the misshapen cushions, the exposed wood of the legs scarred and pitted with age. There was a bin full of children's toys, but nothing in there looked modern. Most of it was old. Well-loved, but faded.

Had he put everything into his business? More than the others? Just how much had he been about to lose when everything got split four ways?

I could certainly see why Tunni and Litr had been so eager to speak in his defense.

Ronnok was just pouring out mugs of coffee at the head of a long table flanked with matching benches. It was large enough to sit two adults and four children, if snugly. One end of the table sat just under a bay window overlooking the back garden, but the walls behind the benches were filled with pinned up examples of the children's art. Layer after layer, like pictures were constantly being added, but nothing was ever taken down.

I saw Esja smile at the sight of it. I found it pretty charming myself. And if none of them were over ten yet, they all looked to have some serious art skills.

I would have to remind her of my earlier plan, that she should teach the children of Villmark art. Not that she had time around her patrolling schedule any more than I did around my volva training.

Still, I just knew she'd be good at it. We had lots of people who could patrol the streets. But teaching art? Not so many could do that.

"The children are with my mother at the moment," Ronnok said as she set a plate piled high with shortbread cookies on the table, then sank down onto one of the benches with a sigh. "If you must, I can take you there to talk with them. But they know even less than I do, and I'd rather not upset them more than they already are."

"I won't talk to the children unless it becomes necessary," I promised her.

She bit her lip, nodding over and over. This moment was about to spin out of control, I could feel it.

She hadn't even seen his body yet. That was the thought that kept coming back to me. She hadn't seen him, trapped in that ice in nothing but his drawers. Head bent over his knees, like he was defeated by exhaustion. Would Brigida bring her to the tent so that she could look into the ice?

She could look, but she couldn't touch. She couldn't even properly see his face. It felt more like torture than comfort. And yet, how long could she go on without seeing him?

The whole situation was so tragically sad. I hated how powerless I felt to make anything any better for this woman.

Then there was a knock on the front door. The others had arrived.

It was time for me to get to work.

CHAPTER FIFTEEN

Roarr led the other two couples into the kitchen. Oda and Arnóra went to Ronnok at once. She had moved from the table to the stove, although there was nothing for her to do there. She just hovered uncertainly until her friends reached her side, pulling her into a tight hug.

There were quiet murmurs of words, and less quiet tears. I stared down at the coffee and shortbread, never wanting either less in my entire life.

But then Ronnok took command of the situation, getting Oda and Arnóra settled at the table. Tunni and Litr approached the table long enough to take mugs of coffee, then retreated closer to the door where Roarr stood leaning against the frame, hands buried deep in his pockets.

Esja and I sat down across from the three women, and I felt everyone's eyes on me as I took out my sketchbook and pencils.

"I have to ask you some questions, and while you answer, I will likely be drawing. I might draw your portraits, or I might draw an image sparked by something you tell me. But I don't want you to focus on what I'm doing. Just on what your answers are. Is that all right?" I asked.

"Of course," Ronnok said.

"Okay," I said, sitting back on my bench so that I could prop my sketchbook up at a drawing angle against the edge of the table. I took up a pencil, but I only held it in my hand, twirling it a little between my fingers. "I met you all, kind of, when you were petitioning the council of three to aid in dissolving your business. But we lacked formal introductions. I guess you know I'm Ingrid Torfudottir."

"Yes, volva," Ronnok said.

"Ingrid is fine," I said.

"I'm Oda, and this is Arnóra," Oda, the woman sitting on the far left across from me, said. "Ronnok, you already know. My husband, Tunni, is the taller one by the door. And that's Arnóra's husband Litr."

I gave everyone nods of greeting. The men I was sure I had straight from before, but the women had been in a group at the back of the room. And aside from not being actual blood relatives, they did look enough alike to pass as sisters. It was good to get the names straight before I started talking.

"And you've all known each other since forever," I said. "You men have been running a business together for years now?"

"Yes," Tunni said. "And we'll still need help with evaluating the worth of everything so we can make a fair split of our assets."

"That's still going to happen," I told him. "I had a friend that was coming up to Villmark to look at your equipment, but that's been delayed for obvious reasons."

"The wall," Tunni said.

"Yes. It's interfering with my phone as well. I can't call or text anyone."

"No one in Villmark has a working phone currently," Litr said.

"You've checked?" I asked. Because it wasn't something *I* had thought to verify if it wasn't just my phone affected.

He traded a glance with Tunni. "We were trying to get ahold of Alfvin, to tell him what happened. But neither of our phones worked. And that's when I tried to find anyone at all with a working phone."

"You wanted to call Alfvin to tell him about Dufnall?" I asked.

"Yes. So that was just this morning," Litr said. "But when I asked others about their phones, they told me they were sure no one else could make calls either."

"I'm sure that's true," I said. Because he was sounding a touch defensive, although I didn't know why. "How did you think Alfvin would respond to the news?"

"What do you mean?" Litr asked, equal parts puzzled and irritated. "We're all devastated. Dufnall was like a brother to him as well as us. He'd want to know as soon as possible. Even if he's trapped on the other side of this wall of ice and can't possibly help out in any way. I gather we can't even get to his body?"

"No," I admitted. "Not until we can find a way to break into the ice."

"But we're working on it," Roarr said. "The whole town. We'll figure it out."

Litr made a skeptical sort of sound, but then buried his face into his mug, taking a long drink of coffee.

"I know what you're probably thinking," Tunni said to me. I raised an eyebrow at him, inviting him to go on. "Well, the four of us are parting ways after decades of working together. And we needed help in working out the best way to do that. Maybe you thought there were bad feelings among us because of that."

"Honestly? The four of you struck me as feeling stressed, but not angry," I said, idly turning back the pages of my sketchbook to the drawing I had done of the four of them. "Alfvin is standing a bit apart from the rest of you, but if I understand correctly, he was the impetus for ending the business."

"It was something we'd talked about before," Litr said, to my surprise.

"Really?"

"This is a small town. There's only so much work to go around. It's really not enough to keep four of us occupied any longer," Tunni said.

"Nearly every family in Villmark has at least one of our pieces in it," Litr added.

"So you've saturated the market," I said.

"Tunni and I have talked about setting up a business selling our work to the outside world," Litr said.

"Dufnall wouldn't hear of it," Ronnok put in. "He wanted to run the business as a Villmarker only business. And he wanted our children to apprentice under him when they're older."

"So he was going to carry on working in his father's workshop?" I asked.

"He hoped to," she said. "It would depend on how much cash we ended up with after everything was split four ways. If we could afford to pay for everyone else's shares in the equipment."

"We were working on a plan to support that," Tunni said.

"There's no reason why Tunni and I couldn't share the equipment with Dufnall. Come up with some kind of schedule for access," Litr said.

"We were just waiting to find out how much we'd have to sell outright to pay Alfvin his share," Tunni said.

"So, no bad feelings there?" I asked. I tried to sound neutral, not skeptical. But I'm not sure I succeeded.

"Not at all," Tunni said.

"We know how things have been going for Njorun's family," Oda said. "They've had a tough time. She and Alfvin moving out of Villmark and back to the farm to support her parents, that's not anything we'd ever stand in the way of."

"Dufnall dying has nothing to do with either of them," Ronnok said firmly. "And it has nothing to do with the business."

"You're sure of that," I said. Not quite a question.

She just nodded curtly and took one of the squares of shortbread. Not that she ate it. But crumbling it between her fingers seemed to lend her some measure of comfort.

"We're all sure of that," Oda said, laying her hand on Ronnok's arm.

"Okay," I said. I started idly drawing on my sketchbook, just a warmup of lines and shapes. Nothing serious yet. "Ronnok, can you tell me what happened last night? The patrols are quite sure that Dufnall wasn't where they found him when they'd passed that point before. So he must've been outside quite late."

"Last night was normal," Ronnok said, still crumbling her square of shortbread. She was very studious about it, like she needed to be sure every single crumb was the same size as all the others. "The kids were excited about the ice wall, of course. Not scared. I think they thought the cold meant snow was coming, and were looking forward to that. But of course the sky was clear all day."

She sighed and looked around the room, as if looking for triggers to help her memory. "We had dinner together like we always do. Beef and potato stew. Apple cake. Then Dufnall and I together put all the children to bed. There was the usual demand for drinks of water and just one more story. It always takes longer than it really ought to."

Oda squeezed her hand on Ronnok's arm and gave her a soft smile that Ronnok made a half-hearted attempt to return.

"Then I cleaned up in the kitchen. Dufnall was going to head to the workshop to do some detailing work on a project." Then she sat up straighter, as if something had just occurred to her. "He brought in more firewood first, from the yard. I remember that. He came in with an armful of wood, and he was kind of humming or whistling something. It was a tune… I can't remember the name of it now, but it was so familiar. I was only half paying attention. I'm sorry, I can't remember what it was now. Not the name or the tune to hum it for you."

"That's all right," I said. The image emerging under my pencil now was capturing that scene: Ronnok washing up after dinner and Dufnall coming into the kitchen with an armful of wood. It was a cozy little scene, actually. It would make a lovely pen and ink illustration.

Not that I could bear to work it up like I was going to sell it. That felt wrong. Like selling someone else's happiness. Or their sorrow.

"Was it coming from the wall, do you think?" Arnóra asked.

"What do you mean?" Ronnok asked with a confused furrow to her brow.

"Well, other people in town say they've heard singing coming from the wall," Arnóra said. "Like women singing, is what I've heard. Too distant for words to be clear. But apparently it's quite alluring."

"No, I don't think that was it at all," Ronnok said. "Alluring? No. It was jaunty, like something we'd dance to as kids." She closed her eyes and I could see her working hard to summon up that half-remembered melody again. But she had to give up with a sigh.

"He went outside to fetch wood from your own garden," I pointed out. "That's nowhere near the wall."

"That's right," Ronnok said. She sounded like she was grateful for my words.

"And afterwards, he went to his workshop? That's in the marketplace, right? Just two blocks south of here? Also nowhere near the wall?" I went on.

"That's right," she said again. "Whatever brought that song to mind, I don't think he heard it coming from the wall. And if he thought he had, wouldn't he have said so to me?"

"Would he?" Arnóra wondered. "I mean, if it really was a voice trying to lure him away, like a voice from a siren, would he tell you about that?"

"He wasn't lured away," Ronnok said almost forcefully.

"I've heard the rumors about the singing," I said. "But not from the patrols. Not from anyone who's actually been close to the wall. I can't say for sure, of course, but I think this is just a rumor. People are nervous. Understandably."

"Dufnall wasn't lured away," Ronnok said. "He went to finish up a job."

"And you went to bed?" Esja asked. "Before he returned?"

"He said he'd likely be late, so yes," Ronnok said. "And when I woke in the morning, he wasn't there. He had never come home. Which doesn't happen often, but *does* happen. Especially with how cold it was outside last night, it made sense that he had decided just to sleep by the fire in the workshop and come home after the sun was up. Not that it got any warmer then."

No, it was as bitterly cold as ever out there. And it was late enough in the afternoon now that it was starting to get dark again as well. And who knew what this night might bring?

I looked down at my drawing. I could sense the music in the lines and shading around Dufnall's figure. But there was nothing sinister there. There was a bouncing quality to the lines around him, but a merry one. My impression was the same as Ronnok's, of something jaunty and danceable. Not something like a siren would sing to lure him to his doom.

And yet, at some point after leaving his wife's side, he had done just that. He had gone for some inexplicable reason to the ice wall, stripped down to his underthings, and sat down to let the ice swallow him.

That certainly felt like a luring situation.

"I need to see the workshop next, I think," I said, closing my sketchbook. "Then I might need to talk to you all again. I know the patrols are watching over you all?"

"Two of them are waiting for us outside right now," Tunni told me.

"Us too. But we should really get home to our children now, Ingrid," Arnóra said with a quick glance at Litr. "I mean, if you're leaving to look at the workshop, that is. We can talk with you again if you need to. You can call on us at home."

"Thank you," I said. "I definitely don't want to keep you from your children."

"Tunni and I left our children with their cousins. We haven't told them about Dufnall yet. They're only four and five. They think they're having a party with their cousins," Oda said. She wrapped an arm around Ronnok and gave her another tight squeeze. "I'll be staying here, Ronnok. And I won't take no for an answer."

"I wouldn't dream of trying to tell you no," Ronnok said fondly. Then she got up from the table, crossing the kitchen to a bowl on the corner of the worktable beside the stove. She came back with a single iron key and pressed it into my hand. "For the workshop."

"Thank you," I said, sliding it into my pocket. I tried to find a way to say that I hoped seeing that space would help me figure out what happened to Dufnall, but I couldn't find a way to say that which wasn't too close to the truth.

Which was that it would really help if the workshop had been the actual scene of the crime.

I mean, there was still a sliver of a chance that it had been some kind of accident, and not a murder. Particularly as everyone kept declaring the innocence of my only real suspect.

I stood there too long, I fear. Just opening and closing my mouth and fidgeting with the sketchbook in my hands.

But Roarr came to my rescue, taking me by the elbow to guide me towards the door. "We have a few other stops to make before it's full dark out there, so we should really hurry," he said.

"We do?" I hissed to him the instant we were out of the kitchen and in the hall.

He just shrugged, then handed me my coat.

I guessed I had looked more at sea than even I had thought. But I could always trust Roarr to throw me a line.

I was starting to rely on that a lot these days.

CHAPTER SIXTEEN

Esja parted ways from Roarr and me the minute we stepped out of Ronnok's house, eager to volunteer for what was surely going to be extra patrols that night. As much as I would really prefer to keep her in my sight, I couldn't come up with a single valid reason to force her to. Nothing strange had been happening with her since the moment at the bonfire. She didn't seem to be going through any kind of changes.

Roarr had caught my eye and gave a shake of his head, letting me know he hadn't seen anything either. Although when she skipped away from us towards the commons, I could tell from the way he watched her disappear into the growing gloom of evening that his urge to keep her close at hand was even stronger than mine.

But we had to let her go. Not least because we really did have other things to do.

He and I spent an hour inside the workshop so I could draw the space from different angles. But by the time we called it quits, nothing about our first impression from the moment we'd walked in the door into the chilled space had changed.

Dufnall had never made it here the night before. There was no sign he had turned on any of the lights, touched any of the tools, or even brought the heat back up from its lowest setting.

I supposed he could've come in and left again, turning off the lights and bringing the heat back down before he'd left and locking the door again on his way out. But the entire space had an emptiness to it. My gut reaction said he hadn't been here, and nothing I drew from any angle changed that impression.

Whatever had happened to him, it had either happened before he'd arrived, or after he tried to get home again. My money was on before he'd arrived.

Which left me bitterly disappointed. I had really been banking on finding a pile of clothes here, at the very least. So far, no one had seen a stitch of any of his garments anywhere.

"We should eat," Roarr said as we walked together through the dark streets. "I'll go back out on my own afterwards to check my markers before I go to bed."

"And if your path should cross Esja's?" I said, not quite teasing him.

"I'll just make sure she's still doing okay," he said. "At this point, she's not quite stronger than I am, but she's definitely a better fighter. The Mikkelsens have taught her to defend herself. Maybe too well."

"You could always ask her for lessons. If you wanted to narrow the gap," I said.

He huffed out a laugh under his breath. "Yeah, that's not me."

"No, you definitely have a different calling," I agreed.

Neither of us felt much like cooking, so we headed to Ullr's mead hall instead. I was surprised to find it packed, although I wasn't quite sure why. Of course the people of Villmark would feel better in groups. And with Aldis' mead hall on the other side of the ice wall, this place was already guaranteed to do twice the business.

But I sensed no one wanted to be alone that night. It reminded too many of us of the month before, when being alone had been a real danger.

Being alone had meant potentially being a victim. But it had also turned out to mean potentially being the killer. Or a tool of the killer. Either way, there was safety in numbers. And maybe that was true this time, too.

Roarr and I ate without talking. Roasted chicken with root vegetables and the last of the season's fresh herbs. It was warm and filling, but I couldn't quite taste any of it. Partly I was too distracted, turning over the pages of my sketchbook and desperately hoping to see something I had missed before.

But also, I think spending even just a single hour with Ronnok had brought up memories of my own grief. My mother had died the summer before. Just over a year ago. It was a million years ago, sometimes.

But other times, it was like yesterday. And today was definitely one of those times.

Roarr walked me back to our front door without me even really noticing he was doing it. It was only when he hesitated there, holding the door open to let me in first, that I noticed him watching me with something like worry in his eyes. "Are you going to be okay?"

"I'm fine," I told him. "I'm going to close this book for now and put it away," I added, gesturing at him with the sketchbook. "I might take a minute to try to refocus on my current rune, but maybe not. I think I just need to sleep."

To sleep, and to hope that I wasn't woken before dawn again with another knock on the door.

With another body of a fellow Villmarker to go look at.

"If you're sure?" he said with deep skepticism.

"Check the markers," I told him, giving him a little push away from the door. "It's important. Esja was only half teasing about the numbers in your notebook. She knows it could be important too. Go get your numbers. You can peek in at me if you need to be reassured when you get back. But I'm really hoping I see the sun in the morning before I see you or anyone else."

"Yes," he said with a grave nod. He took two slow steps backwards, away from the door, before finally giving in and turning to walk away from me.

I did indeed put the sketchbook away, leaving it downstairs before I even went up to brush my teeth.

I didn't bother trying to connect with Iss, however. I was just too tired. I fell face-first onto my pillow, at first grateful that Mjolner wasn't there to object to my pillow-hogging and then worried that I still hadn't seen him.

And then I was deeply asleep, lost in a world of gray clouds and white snow. I could hear the soft whistle of the wind, distant, as if my dream-self was wearing a hood pulled tight over a wool cap with snug ear flaps.

But I could also hear the soft shush-shush of skis over snow. A cross-country skier, making good time. But no matter which way I turned, all I saw were clouds and unmarred snow. The skier never came into view. I just kept turning and turning.

A frustrating dream, to be sure.

Interrupted, inevitably, by a knock on my front door. And when I turned over and opened my eyes, all I saw was the darkness of my middle-of-the-night bedroom.

By this time, I could almost get downstairs in my sleep. Left foot slipper, right foot slipper, hoodie on and zipped up to my throat. Shuffle down the stairs.

To find Roarr already dressed and standing at the open door, talking again with Skefill.

But this time Esja was there too, standing at Skefill's elbow. Her cheeks were bright red, from the cold and the emotion of the moment too.

"Who?" was all I said.

"Tunni," Skefill told me. "The same as Dufnall, but in a different location. My patrol is already setting up a tent to hide the area from view."

"Tunni," I said, rubbing at my head. "How is this not related to Dufnall? It can't be random chance."

"No," Roarr agreed. "But we saw him last night."

"We saw him last *afternoon*," I corrected him.

"No, last night," he persisted. "At Ullr's." At my frown, he continued. "Maybe you didn't notice. He was there when we were. He was eating with the two members of the patrol who had been assigned to him. He wasn't alone, is my point. He had two other people with him, people who should've been with him all night."

"Where are they now?" I asked.

"Presumably, still at home," Skefill said. "I have men heading there now."

Esja scowled at his word choice. It was quite the scowl. Skefill seemed to feel it even with Esja standing behind him, completely out of view from him in the depths of his fur-lined hood.

"I have members of my patrol heading there now," he amended, then cleared his throat awkwardly.

I was too stunned to respond to that. I had been so worried about his potential influence on Esja, it had never occurred to me to take into account the reverse. That she was rubbing off on him.

"They'll check in with you when they know?" Roarr asked, even as he reached for his coat. "Because we should get to the body first."

"Yes," Skefill said.

"Let me grab my art bag," I said, heading back into the darkness of my living room before starting to put on my boots. I was getting used to this early start to my days, apparently. Not that I liked it any more.

Not remotely.

Although the view of the village out my window was breathtaking. There was still no moon, but there were also no clouds in the sky. And the stars seemed unusually bright, lighting up the ring of ice wall in a brilliant sparkle of bluish-silver. I could just make out bits of it here and there between the buildings, but mostly I saw the aura reflecting off of it.

"Is it glowing?" I asked as I rejoined the others.

"You mean the wall? No more than usual," Skefill said. "Why? Do you think something is happening to it?"

"I don't know," I said, trying not to sound surly. "Ask me again when I'm actually looking at the thing."

My attitude didn't bother him. He just shrugged and waited as I struggled into my boots and parka. I grabbed my hat, scarf and gloves to put on as we walked.

"Did Valki double the patrols?" I asked as I followed Skefill. East this time. Almost exactly due east, towards the end of town by the birch trees and the meadow.

"Not officially," Esja told me. "He didn't have to. There was an abundance of volunteers."

Which fit with my sensation of the night before sitting in Ullr's mead hall. No one wanted to be alone. And I wasn't the only one losing sleep over all this.

"It was the same as with Dufnall," Skefill said. "The patrols had been by this area before, and there was no sign of any trouble. But the last patrol to pass by saw him already covered in ice. He's unreachable."

"He's also undressed and sitting with his head bent over his knees," Esja said. "He never saw Dufnall, did he?"

"I would have to check with Brigida, but I don't think she's even let Ronnok see the body yet," I said. Brigida, in addition to being a member of the council of three, was also the person in Villmark who took charge of all our dead. She helped the families prepare the bodies for burial. This sort of thing was totally her area.

"Ingrid," Roarr said, hurrying his steps to reach my side. "I'm going to split off. I want to check the markers. I know it's early yet, but—"

"Go," I told him. "Find me later and tell me what you learn."

"Absolutely," he said, and jogged off, back a block to the main road and then turning to follow it to the north end of town.

"More people are talking about the singing," Skefill told me.

"What people?" I asked. Perhaps a bit too harshly. I took a breath, then tried again. "Because I've gotten the impression that no one on a patrol has heard this singing. Esja, Roarr and I haven't. You haven't?" I lifted that up ever so slightly into a question, and when he shook his head, I went on. "I don't think anyone with the wall running in their back garden has heard it. So who has?"

"To be honest, I haven't heard anyone tell me they've heard it themselves," Esja said. "It's always they heard from someone else who heard this singing."

"Skefill—" I started to say.

"I'll have the patrols pass word around," he interrupted me to say. "If we can find a single person who's heard this music for themselves, I will send them to you."

"Thank you, Skefill," I said.

He just nodded, then pointed to the wall just emerging into view in the predawn darkness ahead of us.

The tent was already set up in front of the frozen body, and when we ducked inside, it was to find the interior brightly lit and almost too warm. There were four braziers inside, each blazing intensely.

I unzipped my coat and pulled off my hat, but kept my gloves on as I approached the wall of ice.

Despite the heat from the braziers, it was as glazed slick as ever. It wasn't sweating, not even a little bit.

And in its blue depths, I could just make out the shadow of Tunni, sitting as if against a wall, head bent over his drawn-up knees. Wearing nothing but his undershorts.

"Two like this can't be paradoxical undressing," Skefill said.

"No," I agreed.

"Something is doing this," he said.

"Or someone," I said.

But I knew, if I couldn't figure out who that "someone" is, the "something" theory was going to gain ground. And without knowing what the "something" was, terror was going to grow.

And I didn't really need Roarr to come back with numbers to know the ice wall had taken another meter of radius away from us already. I could tell from where Tunni's back seemed to be resting against the prior iteration of the wall.

We were running out of space. And we were running out of time.

CHAPTER SEVENTEEN

I STAYED IN THE TENT, drawing Tunni over and over again, but it was hard to focus. I had no hope of getting into any kind of flow state. The headache that was building pressure behind my eyes was making it too hard even to think. It was all I could do to keep the pencil moving over the paper.

I gave up with barely disguised relief when Brigida arrived with the dawn. She went straight to the ice wall and peered inside, then turned to look at me, first with a fierce anger but then with a softer pity.

I think I liked the anger better.

"I don't know," was all I could say.

"You haven't been sleeping," she said. Not a question.

But I shook my head. "I've been getting up early, but I *have* been sleeping. I've been crashing hard the minute my head hits the pillow."

She looked at me skeptically. Then she stepped closer, grasping my chin to turn my face closer to the light of the brazier beside me. "You've not been sleeping well." Again, not a question. But she raised one eyebrow at me, like she was open to hearing an answer.

"I would say I'm getting about six hours of sleep without waking up that I can remember," I said.

"But?" she prompted.

"But I *do* feel exhausted," I admitted.

She chewed at her lip for a moment. "Haraldr tells me sometimes you use your dreams to do your magic."

"It's not so much magic as..." But I trailed off. I didn't want to have a long discussion about what it meant, to establish a relationship with each rune, one at a time. So I just shrugged and said, "Sometimes it's like magic. But that isn't what I've been doing lately. Not that I haven't tried. It would be great to get an answer to what's going on here. And I am supposed to be working on my current rune with Haraldr. Either one, a little dream work would be great right now."

"You haven't been dreaming at all?" she asked.

"Well," I said. Then I found myself trailing off again.

"What have you been dreaming?" she pressed.

"Nothing, really," I said. "Just a recurring scrap of a dream. I'm standing in a snowy landscape, and I can hear skis approaching. Someone is skiing towards me. But I always wake up before I see anything. Honestly, I've had way more intense dreams than that in the past. There's nothing about that which should be making me so tired."

"And yet," she said, ending her sentence with a gentle uplift of her hand towards my apparently visibly exhausted face.

"I don't think it means anything," I said. "It's not an answer to any of my questions."

"I wish your grandmother were here," she said wistfully.

"No one wishes that more than I do," I said.

"That wasn't a slight on you, dear," she said. "And I know she's said a thousand times that divination isn't her thing. Still. She might know what approaching skis mean."

I said nothing.

"Try getting a nap today," she suggested.

"But I should talk to Oda again, and the others. Right?" I asked.

"I'll break the news to all of them," she said. "Do you think it's likely you'll see something today that you didn't see when you spoke with them all yesterday?"

"Maybe?" I said. But I knew I didn't sound remotely convincing.

"Nap," she said, pointing a commanding finger at me. "Then, maybe take a patrol tonight if you're feeling up for it. You've been wearing yourself out drawing this wall from every angle, but always by day. It looks different at night. Maybe you should try that."

Which was far too sensible of a suggestion for me to ignore. I was a little bit mad I hadn't thought of it myself.

I honestly don't know who walked me home again. I know someone was there, at least up to my door.

It was a good thing I was mostly in my pajamas already, as I collapsed the minute I reached the edge of my bed. I still had socks and my hoodie on as I once more face-planted on the bed and immediately fell into a deep sleep.

But not a dreamless one. If you could call the never-ending loop of the approaching skis scene a dream.

I had had better ones.

At least when I woke up this time, it was to find my room filled with sunlight. Granted, it was the last light from the setting sun. But it was that golden warmth that had woken me, not another knock on my door.

I dressed, made a half-hearted attempt at brushing out my hair, then headed downstairs to find Roarr and Esja both in the kitchen. Roarr was poring over the columns of numbers in his notebook, but Esja hopped up at once, reaching into the oven and pulling out a bowl of tomato soup and a plate of grilled cheese sandwiches that had been left to keep warm there.

My stomach growled at once. I had missed breakfast. And lunch. At least my dinner the night before had been a late one, if one I had only picked at.

"Brigida assigned me to patrol with you," Esja informed me as she slid back into her chair and reached for the mug of tea she had left there. "Roarr is coming too, aren't you, Roarr?"

Roarr made a noncommittal noise. I just busied myself with getting the food inside me as quickly as I could. Which was kind of a shame. Roarr made a mean grilled cheese, and as much as they were better fresh from the cast-iron pan, even after being kept warm in the oven for who knows how long they were still too delicious to be eaten the way I was, chewing and swallowing so fast I could scarcely taste anything.

"It's shrinking faster," Roarr said at last, shutting his notebook with a sigh. "No matter how I work the numbers, that's a fact."

"Each time it shrinks, the circle gets smaller. So the amount of ice needed to take off another meter of radius is less than before," I said.

"I know. I took that into account," he said.

"I promise you he did," Esja added with a wink.

"It's shrinking faster," he said. "The markers I put out at dawn? I expect to find we've lost more than two meters when I check them again at dawn tomorrow."

"It's going to start reaching houses soon," I said.

"It's already encroached on a lot of gardens," Roarr said. "Dog kennels, chicken coops, rabbit hutches. They've all been swallowed up by the ice."

"No animals yet," Esja quickly added.

"No, just humans," I sighed. I swallowed the last of the tomato soup, then got up from the table. "I'll grab my art bag. We should get out there."

"And do what?" Esja asked.

"See," I said.

Because what else was there? We would walk the perimeter, see that Roarr was right about the thickening wall, and hope we didn't find any more bodies.

The sun was out of sight by the time we stepped out my door, but the gloaming still hung over everything. The air was as chill as ever, but there was no hint of snow. Just a cloudless sky that was gaining stars one silvery pinpoint at a time.

"I'll wait for full dark before I try drawing any of it," I said.

"Do you want to start in one of the tents?" Roarr asked. "It's warmer there."

"I've already tried drawing from inside the tents. I don't think I'll see anything more now than I did before," I said. Although I couldn't help the wistful sigh. Warmer did sound nice.

"North first?" Roarr asked. "I know I'm not checking my markers yet, but that is the closest spot where I've set up."

"Sure," I said. All the directions were the same to me.

Where Roarr had set up his markers was just past the old tree that stood atop the highest point of Villmark. The road north ended under its boughs, a circular path worn around it in the dirt by generations of feet. Fainter paths branched off of that circle, heading northeast towards the shore of the lake and northwest, towards my cabin in the woods.

Or, they would have. But the ice wall had extended past both of those points. It was closing in on the tree itself now. The tree might already be in danger, actually. I had no idea what effect all that ice might have on the tree's root system. But I doubted it could be good.

"Yeah, it's definitely growing already," Roarr said as he bent to examine stakes driven into the hard ground. I couldn't exactly see how he knew this by sight alone, but I trusted him. He had a system.

But then Esja made a sound, something between a sigh and a gasp of surprised excitement.

"What is it?" I asked.

"I don't know," she admitted. "I was just walking along the perimeter of the wall, sort of dragging my fingers against it..." She demonstrated for me, the fingers of her gloved hand dancing over the mirror-like surface of the wall. But I couldn't see what had made her make that noise.

"And?" I prompted.

"It feels different. Just here," she said.

I copied her movements, and she watched me eagerly. But I ended with a shrug.

"You didn't feel it?" she asked, disappointed.

I shook my head. But then I backed up and made a second pass. Then a third, this time with my glove off. The cold of the ice felt like it was sucking every bit of warmth out of my quickly whitening fingers. But there was nothing surprising about that sensation. I put my glove back on and shook my head again.

"What did you feel?" Roarr asked.

"I don't know," Esja said again, maddeningly. But then she made a visible effort to summon more words. "It's like I get a feeling touching that part of the wall."

"Like it's colder? Or warmer?" Roarr asked.

I pressed my hand to the wall, but there was nothing different about it to my senses. It was as cold, as hard, and as scratch-free as any of the rest of the cold, smooth expanse.

"No, it's a *feeling*," Esja insisted. "Like an emotion."

"From the wall," Roarr said. But he wasn't teasing her. Not remotely.

"I feel… happiness?" she said, but then she shook her head. "No, it's like relief. Something here is going to bring relief to someone."

"Going to? Like, in the future?" I said.

Esja put her hand back on the wall and closed her eyes. Her brows furrowed with her concentration. She bit down on her lip, hard enough to draw a single drop of blood.

But when she opened her eyes again, it was just with another shrug then shake of her head. "I don't know. I don't think I get a sense of time, exactly. Just the feeling. Happy relief. But not *now*."

"Maybe we'll feel it too, then," Roarr said. "When the time comes."

"If it didn't already pass," I said.

"Do you want to mark the spot?" Roarr asked, holding up his stakes and hammer.

"No, I'll remember it," Esja said with total confidence. "But Ingrid, maybe you should try drawing here first?"

"It is convenient, with the bench under the tree and all," I admitted.

I drew there, working with my gloves off for as long as I was able to at a time. But my drawings showed me nothing.

We walked on throughout the night, stopping at the cardinal points to check Roarr's markers, but stopping even more frequently for me to draw other sections of the wall.

When the wall was closer to people's homes, I did get some imagery in the background of my drawings. But they were all of trepidation. People's fear. Everyone's growing claustrophobia.

Nothing I didn't know already.

It was far past midnight, as we were just approaching Roarr's southern-most marker location, when I saw a figure coming toward us from the center of town. I knew from his gait that it was Skefill, walking alone this time.

And I knew before he even opened his mouth what he was about to report to me.

Litr. Litr was the wall's latest victim.

Most maddening of all, we didn't have to walk far to get to where the patrol was already setting up a third tent.

Because Roarr, Esja and I had just been there fifteen minutes before. And there had been no sign of a body there then.

But there was no question there was one there now.

CHAPTER EIGHTEEN

THERE DIDN'T SEEM to be much point in lingering there near the wall. I didn't even wait for Brigida to arrive. Skefill and his patrol didn't need my direction to do what was necessary to preserve the scene.

But with every added tent, it became less and less likely that people didn't know what we were hiding from view. Especially not with the way rumors carried through Villmark.

It was the bitterest of hopes that this would be the last. With Alfvin on the other side of the wall, there was no business partner left to be a victim. But with the three of them being taken one by one, and no one else affected, the idea that this wasn't about their business somehow was becoming impossible to countenance.

So Roarr, Esja and I only made the briefest of visits to the latest crime scene. Litr's body was just as buried behind ice as the other two, just as impossible to reach or even see clearly. His position was the same, and he was stripped down to his shorts just as the other two had been.

There was nothing more for me to learn here.

I hadn't gone to see Tunni's wife Oda after he had disappeared. It hadn't seemed necessary. Tunni had walked out of a mead hall he was in with their protective patrol, and no one had seen him after until his body was found. It seemed very unlikely she knew or had seen anything that the two members of the patrol who had actually been with Tunni at the time hadn't known or seen. And they had been thoroughly questioned. Me asking her all the same questions was just added stress I hadn't thought she needed.

But now that it was all three men dead, I needed to get the widows together one more time. There must be something we were missing, some hint or clue or connection I hadn't found yet.

I would just have to keep asking questions until I got to the right question. The one that would unlock… something.

My hopes were wispy, fragile things. Basically, the total opposite of the wall of ice closing in around us all.

Roarr and Esja went with me to Litr's house to speak to Arnóra first. Skefill had already sent someone to fetch Ronnok and Oda and bring them to me there. But, as it wasn't quite dawn yet, I expected it would take some time for them to arrive.

Which was fine. The patrol who had been watching her house overnight were still there, and as much as I knew Valki had already grilled them both, I wanted to talk to them as well. I had plenty to do, if not enough sleep to do it particularly efficiently.

One of the members of the patrol opened the door at our knock, then led us into the kitchen, where the other patrol member was sitting with a wrecked-looking Arnóra. She was dressed in her night things with a thick, hooded bathrobe tied snugly around her. There was a mug of what I took to be tea sitting in front of her, but as much as she kept starting to reach for it, its contents were untouched and no longer steaming.

"Arnóra," I said as I came into the room, followed by Esja. Roarr stayed in the doorway, leaning one shoulder against the frame. This house wasn't much bigger than the one shared by Dufnall and Ronnok, although with two fewer children, its snug interiors weren't quite so cluttered.

I sat down across from her and reached across the table to squeeze one of her hands from where it was resting, not quite touching that tea. "I'm sorry for your loss."

She nodded mutely and wiped at her eyes before throwing an imploring look at the patrolwoman sitting beside her at the table.

"Ingrid Torfudottir, I can tell you everything that happened here, or as much of it as the three of us know. If it helps. Arnóra has had a rough morning, and since her version of events mostly coincides with mine, I can do the talking," she said.

"That's fine with me," I said, taking out my sketchbook and pencil. I glanced over at Arnóra. "You'll jump in if you need to correct or add anything?"

Arnóra just nodded again. As if speaking was more than she had the energy for at the moment.

"Go ahead…" I trailed off, realizing I didn't know the name of the woman I was speaking to. I'd seen her a few times before. She wasn't a close friend of the Mikkelsens, but she knew them well enough to trade words with them if they met on the street.

"Kolla," she said, with a smile that said there were no hard feelings.

"Kolla," I repeated. "You were on duty here since last night?"

"Yes. Darri and I have been here since sunset," she said, with a nod towards the man who had let us in the front door. He was at the stove, waiting for a kettle to come to boil, and didn't react to the sound of his name. "The previous watch had nothing to report, so we settled in for our shift in the living room. Darri and I had already eaten before coming here, so when the family sat down for dinner, despite their kind invitation, we didn't eat with them."

"That's significant?" I asked.

"We think it might be," Kolla said. "We think something was in the stew."

"The last of it is still here, on the back of the stove," Darri put in. "We covered the pan and kept it, but I don't know what good that will do. It smells fine, and it looks fine."

"But neither of us wanted to taste it to know for sure," Kolla said.

And it wasn't like even without a wall of ice we had a forensics lab we could send it to. Not that I wanted to bring that up. But I felt they were both dancing around it.

"What do you think was in the stew?" I asked.

"Maybe nothing," Kolla said, shooting a look at Arnóra as if asking for her confirmation. But, again, Arnóra just shrugged. "Well, the thing is, Arnóra seemed well when Darri and I arrived. But by the time the family was finishing up dinner, she was practically falling asleep at the table. Darri and Litr had to help her up the stairs to her bed." She gave Arnóra another concerned look. "She said she didn't feel ill exactly. Just tired."

"It's been a trying couple of days," I put in.

Arnóra nodded again.

"So, you think there was something in the stew that put her to sleep?" I asked, looking from Kolla to Darri. "But then why didn't Litr fall asleep too? And what about the children?"

"The children are still asleep, even now," Kolla said. "They're breathing normally, but we can't wake them."

Arnóra's head dropped until the tangles of her hair were covering her face. But I saw tears drop down onto the surface of her tea.

"Their grandmother is with them," Kolla quickly added at my look of alarm. "She works in the greenhouse and public gardens and has some knowledge of medicinal plants. She has a list of things she thinks might be in the stew, which is why we kept it. But she's confident the children will wake on their own in a few more hours."

"This is horrifying," I said, staring down at the blank page before me. I had yet to sketch a single thing. "Someone poisoned your entire family?"

"Not poison," Arnóra said. Her voice sounded crackly. Like she hadn't used it to make sounds in years. "Just something to make us sleep."

"But Litr wasn't affected?" I asked.

"He didn't eat much," Kolla said. "He was preoccupied."

Which, given he had lost two friends in as many days, was totally understandable. And yet. If I didn't know for a fact he was dead and frozen, trapped inside an ice wall blocks from here, I would consider him a prime suspect in what happened to the rest of his family.

"So Darri and Litr brought Arnóra upstairs and put her to bed," I said, forcing my pencil to make a few lines across the page. The outline of the kitchen around me took shape, vaguely. "Then, I'm guessing, the children as well. Then what happened?"

"Litr was in the kitchen cleaning up after dinner," Kolla said, pausing to give Darri a quick smile of thanks as he put a fresh mug of tea on the table in front of her. "Then he went upstairs himself. We assumed he was up there, sleeping the same as the rest of them. Until one of Skefill's boys came knocking on the door. We didn't hear him leave. And we had a clear view of both of the doors out of the house, but we didn't see him."

"They tell me they never dozed off, not even for a minute," Arnóra said in the tiniest of voices. She still had her face aimed down over her tea, and I couldn't see her expression at all.

"We were vigilant," Kolla said. There was a carefulness to her tone, like she was working hard not to sound offended. But at least she was succeeding.

"Why do you think that's significant, Arnóra?" I asked her. "They already said they didn't have any of the stew. They weren't dosed with whatever you and the children ate."

"I don't know if it was the stew," Arnóra said, pushing back her hair to look at me with glassily dry eyes. "It didn't feel like medicine making me sleep. It felt like what happened the other night. When the wall appeared. When the whole village was asleep."

"But all of us woke up at pretty much the same time when that happened," Kolla said. "And the children upstairs are still sleeping. They won't wake up no matter how much we shake them. It's not the same at all."

Arnóra's mouth twisted into an angry scowl, but she went back to saying nothing.

"This is why it's important that you two were awake the whole night," I said to Kolla and Darri. "If it was the same magic as before, you should've been affected, too."

"The whole town would be, wouldn't it?" Kolla asked.

"I don't know what happened, or how it worked," I admitted.

"Still, we were watching the doors, and we were watching each other," Darri said, crossing his arms from where he was leaning against the now-cold stove. "We were awake the entire night."

"But you didn't see Litr go out," I said. "And we know that he did. I've seen him myself."

"If something had come into our bedroom and snatched him from our very bed, I wouldn't have felt a thing," Arnóra said miserably. "I would've slept through anything."

"It took a bit to wake her up to give her the news," Kolla said. "But once her eyes were open, she was awake. There wasn't any lingering grogginess."

"You sound like you think it was magic and not medicinal herbs as well now," I said.

"I'm just describing what happened as best I can," she said, lifting her chin ever so slightly as if my words had been a challenge. "I leave the conclusion-drawing to you."

She said that last with a gesture towards my sketchbook. Which had the world's worst rendition of Arnóra's kitchen in pencil and nothing else. Nothing useful. Not that Kolla could see it from the angle I was holding it, but still.

I wouldn't describe what I was currently doing as anything like drawing conclusions. I could barely formulate the questions.

"Did Litr have any reason to go out last night?" I asked. "Dufnall went out to the workshop to finish a project, but no one knows why Tunni ended up outside of that mead hall instead of going back to his table after visiting the restroom. What about Litr?"

"He didn't say much," Darri said. "But I felt like if he needed something, he would've said something to Kolla and me. He didn't resent us being here. Quite the opposite. He was preoccupied, sure. But he was grateful we were here. He wouldn't have sneaked out without checking with us first. If there was somewhere he needed to go, he would've told us so we could get an escort for him."

"That's a lot of reading someone else's thoughts from a single evening together," Kolla said, mildly chastising her partner. But then she clearly felt compelled to add, "But I agree. I don't think he ditched us. I think something lured him away."

Which was possibly the very last word I wanted to hear anyone say. Again. Lured.

And yet, what other possibility was left?

CHAPTER NINETEEN

Ronnok and Oda arrived together, accompanied by their own escorts. Kolla and Darri both hopped up to make coffee for everyone, and one of the new arrivals was sent out to buy fresh rolls from whichever of the bakeries opened first in the morning.

Roarr gave Arnóra his arm to guide her into the living room, where Ronnok and Oda were already settling onto one of the two faded sofas. Esja was chasing the other patrol members into the kitchen, which was really too small to contain them all.

But the same could be said of the living room with the three widows plus Roarr, Esja and me. With Ronnok and Oda on one sofa and Roarr and Arnóra on the other, I took a seat on the hearth of the fireplace that sat between them. Esja took Roarr's former position, standing in the doorway to the kitchen and leaning on the frame with one shoulder as she watched over us all with her arms crossed.

I opened to a fresh page in my sketchbook and turned to Ronnok first. "I know we talked about this before, but tell me the whole story again. From the beginning."

She nodded, took a deep breath while she gathered her thoughts, then started from the moment Dufnall went out to fetch the wood for the fire.

Her story was the same as before, and the sketch I made of that cozy family moment was only different from the first in small artistic choices. Nothing with the potential to bust open the case was even hinted at anywhere in the lines.

Still, it was better than I had managed in the kitchen. I was getting into an artistic flow, anyway, if not a magical one.

Then I turned to Oda, and she told me her story. She and Tunni had parted ways shortly after Roarr, Esja, and I had left Ronnok's house. He had been intending to get something to eat at Ullr's, and she had stayed behind so that Ronnok wouldn't be alone.

"I know Tunni and his guard left right after I did," I said to Oda. "But in those moments before he left, did Tunni seem particularly preoccupied? Was he looking around like he expected to see someone? Or anything unusual at all?"

"No, nothing at all," Oda said.

"Was he singing?" Ronnok asked.

"No," Oda said. "I mean, right before he left, when we were standing in front of your house, we were talking together about what song Dufnall might have been humming, but neither of us even had a guess."

"Litr wasn't singing either," Arnóra said. "Or humming or whistling or anything. And despite what Kolla and Darri said, I don't think he was preoccupied. He was grieving. That's not the same thing."

"No, I agree. It's not," I said.

"Brigida doesn't want us to see the bodies," Ronnok said. "At least, not until someone finds a way to get them out of the wall. Is it... are they... is their condition really so bad?"

I acutely felt the three sets of eyes on me, their silent demand to know what happened to their husbands.

Their despair that they should even have to ask.

"No," I said, chewing at my lip. "It's just..."

But I trailed off. I didn't know what it "just" was.

"There's a sadness to them," Esja said softly from the doorway. "But that sadness was just a moment in time, a flickering of something fleeting, I think. It's only being in the ice, that moment is frozen. It's being stretched far longer in time than it should be."

"It's a distortion," Roarr added. "It feels wrong. Not at peace. I think Brigida is right. Once we get them out of the wall and properly prepared for burial, that's when you should say your last goodbyes. Not now. Not while they're still trapped."

"Trapped in one eternal moment," Esja said.

"All three of them in the same moment?" Oda asked harshly. "On three separate nights? They're all the same?"

"I understand your skepticism," I said. "But the answer is yes. I'm working to understand why, but for now, that's all I can tell you. I'm sure if you insisted, Brigida would give in. But I'm also sure you'd regret it."

"Ingrid, you should show them your drawings," Roarr said. "They'll understand if they see what you drew."

I chewed at my lip even harder than before. I suspected he was right, but I wasn't sure the understanding would be worth the cost.

Because that feeling of those men being trapped in a single moment of sadness, frozen in it for all time? That was exactly what I had been feeling when I had done those drawings. Which didn't help me figure out what happened to them. But it was like a knife of ice to my heart, that feeling. How much worse would it be for these women?

"We would like to see," Ronnok said, and reached out to squeeze my knee. Like I was the one who needed reassurance in this moment.

I just nodded, then turned back the pages of my sketchbook before handing it to her. "That is Dufnall."

She closed her eyes before taking the book from me, positioning it in front of her at the optimal viewing angle before finally, reluctantly, opening her eyes again. She gazed at the image for a long moment, a single tear tracing down her cheek. Then she handed the book back to me with a silent nod of thanks.

"Tunni," I said, turning a few pages before handing the book to Oda. She had been looking over Ronnok's shoulder at the drawing of Dufnall and, prepared by that image, all but snatched the book from my hands to examine my drawing of her own husband. She squinted like she was memorizing every fine detail, even rubbing her fingertip over the paper where the tip of my pencil had left soft indentations.

Then she handed the book back to me.

"Litr," I said, turning to my pages from just hours before. Arnóra looked like she'd rather not take the book from me at all, but when Roarr took it from me and propped it up before her, she looked. Briefly. Then she pressed her hands over her eyes, and Roarr hurriedly handed the book back to me.

I let them have a moment, but mostly because I was preoccupied with my own thoughts. Esja had just defined something I had noticed enough to channel it into my drawing, but hadn't articulated in words.

It did feel like they were trapped in momentary sadness. And it had to be momentary. As much as I had felt the stress they'd all been feeling when they'd petitioned the council of three, none of them had been radiating sadness like this.

And from everything I'd heard since, they had all been basically contented men, fathers of young children and spouses to well-loved women.

So what had happened? Had something triggered this sadness and lured them to the wall? Or had being near the wall triggered the sadness?

I turned back the pages of my sketchbook, looking again at the spot by the tree I had drawn the night before. The spot where Esja had sensed not sadness but happiness. I suddenly wanted to use her as my dousing rod of sorts. I could walk her around the entire perimeter and hunt for spots where she sensed emotions. Maybe we could put up some tents to block off the sad spaces before anyone went near them.

Only, we'd already walked the perimeter. More than once. If she had sensed anything like that before, I knew she would've said something.

So did the spots move? Or flicker on and off?

Or was the spot theory just a red herring? Because if the spots created the sadness, where were their clothes? Did someone clear them away after? Or had they already paradoxically undressed before even getting near the wall?

There was a soft commotion in the room I was only vaguely aware of as I studied my own sketches. Roarr speaking to one of the patrol members then getting up from the couch. Awkward, given the already tight space between the two sofas was dominated by a heavy coffee table he had to work not to crack his knees on.

Then there was a wash of cold air as someone came in through the front door. Which cold air immediately became more welcome when I realized it carried with it the scents of freshly baked cinnamon rolls.

"We should eat," Ronnok said to the other two, and Arnóra started to get up from the sofa. But Roarr, who had circled around behind her in his path to the kitchen door, stopped her with a single hand on her shoulder.

"I've got it," he told her. "Esja is bringing in the coffee. We can take a break from questions for a minute, I think."

He threw a questioning gaze at me with that last, and I quickly nodded my consent. A break with food sounded perfect. And coffee, all the better.

"Esja," I said, motioning for her to approach me after she'd set a tray laden with steaming mugs of coffee on the center of the coffee table. She slipped around the back of the sofa, brushing past Roarr without colliding with the back of Arnóra's head, with all the grace I had seen her deploy in her weapons training.

Handy, that. If I had tried to cross this room when everyone was reaching for coffee, someone somewhere would've ended up with a jostled elbow and an unfortunate stain, if not an outright burn.

"Yes?" she said, leaning close to my ear.

"I want to go out, after this," I told her.

But that was as far as I got in telling her my perimeter-walking plan. Because Roarr returned with a platter stacked high with cinnamon rolls, and the reaction to his return to the sofa was profound.

Not because of the food, although the smell that had been tantalizing coming from inside a covered box coming in the door was downright torturous with the real thing in full view in front of all of us.

And not because of Roarr himself. Not even Arnóra sitting next to him had cast more than a glance his way the whole time they'd been sitting together on the couch.

No, it was something else. Something I didn't quite place at first. All I saw was Roarr setting the platter down and then pulling a thick stack of napkins out of his back pocket to flourish them for anyone to take.

A simple enough gesture. And yet all three of the widows had gone paler than pale. They gawked at him with wide eyes, shrinking back into their respective seats as if they were afraid of what he was about to do.

Which was strange. All he appeared to be doing was offering them food.

It took a moment, but he noticed the change in the mood around him, too. The happy tune he had been humming under his breath died away, followed by the smile in his eyes, and he set the napkins down on the table.

"Is something wrong?" he asked.

"That song," Oda said. "What were you humming just now?"

"Oh. I don't know," Roarr said with an embarrassed flush to his cheeks. "It's just something my mother used to sing when I was little. I don't remember the words, really, but the tune is impossible to get out of your head." Then he laughed, although that laugh conveyed even more shy embarrassment than his cheeks were still showing. "She actually said she hated that song. But it would get stuck in her head, and she'd sing it to get it out again. I guess eventually it worked, because when I got older, I never heard her sing it again."

He ended with an awkward shrug, then worked his way around the sofa to retake his place between Arnóra and my perch on the hearth.

All three women were still staring at Roarr as if they expected him to sprout a second head at any moment. But none of them were explaining their sudden horror.

"Your mother is Ragna Bjorndottir, right?" Oda said at last.

"That's right," Roarr said. He half-reached for one of the cinnamon rolls, but seemed to think better of it when he saw no one else was touching the food. He put his hands on his knees firmly, as if determined to keep them there.

"Ragna," Ronnok said in a dreamy voice. "Ragna, Ragna, Ragna. Oh! I remember her."

"She was a little older than us," Arnóra said. "But she was sometimes there at the bonfires and things. Especially when Riki was playing."

"Well, everyone was there when Riki was playing," Oda said. A merry chuckle tried to bubble up out of her, but died before it truly got started.

"Who's Riki?" Roarr asked before I could get the same words out.

"Oh, Riki," Ronnok said with an even dreamier tone than before. "Riki was a boy our age, back when we were teenagers."

"Everyone loved Riki," Arnóra said.

"I don't know anyone named Riki," Roarr said, throwing a nervous glance my way. Because the only reason Roarr wouldn't know someone in Villmark would be if that someone was no longer alive in Villmark.

"Oh, he left Villmark years ago," Ronnok said. "He could sing, you see. He had a voice like you wouldn't believe. And his songs... Well, they stick with you. As your mother could tell you."

"So what I was just humming now was a Riki song?" Roarr asked, amused.

"Indeed," Ronnok said. "I hadn't thought of that song in ages."

"Me neither," Oda said. "Funny how memory works, isn't it? I haven't heard it since forever, and yet I could sing it beginning to end right now. If my voice was... well, let's just say Riki was never going to hit me up for any duets."

"Riki was too big for Villmark," Arnóra said with a sigh.

"So, what happened to him?" I asked. "An accident? Or an illness?"

"Neither," Ronnok said, finally breaking down and letting herself be the first person to reach for a cinnamon roll. "What happened to him was ambition."

"Huh?" Roarr said.

Again, faster than I could articulate the same question.

"He left Villmark," Oda said, waving her hands around to encapsulate the town around us. "To find his fortune in the great big world. Your world," she added with a wave of a hand in my direction.

I didn't know how to tell them, but I was pretty sure he hadn't succeeded in finding his fortune. Unless he had downgraded his ambitions to something more manageable. Which happens all the time. Far more people want to be rock stars than could ever achieve that goal.

But if anyone named Riki—who must've looked like a Nordic god from the way these women were still getting sparkly-eyed just remembering the teenaged version of him—had ever had a brush with fame, I think I would remember.

"So he just disappeared one day, off to the wide world?" Roarr asked.

"Well," Ronnok said, and looked to the other women around her with a gleam in her eye. "He did stop by to see each of us before he left, didn't he?"

"Not that we knew this about each other. Not for *years*," Oda said.

"He came to each of our windows in the middle of the night to tell us he was leaving to find his fortune," Arnóra said. "Those were his exact words. Finding his fortune."

"Like a fairy tale," I said, but mostly to myself.

"And he made each of us promise to wait for him to return," Ronnok said. Then she laughed. "And what would've happened when he did? Was he expecting to have three wives?"

"We never did agree that it was just the three of us," Oda reminded her. "It could've been half the town for all we know."

"Still," Ronnok said.

"So he promised to return and then he never did?" Roarr asked.

"Well, it's not like I thought he really would," Ronnok said. "I mean, swept up in that moment with him leaning in my bedroom window? I absolutely promised I would wait for him."

"But six months later, she was engaged to Dufnall," Oda said.

"You didn't hold out much longer," Ronnok said.

"He had a real charm to him, that's for sure," Arnóra said. "But it didn't linger. When he wasn't there to keep you dancing to his tune, he was kind of hard to remember."

"I always thought that was because he left," Ronnok said, her tone suddenly quiet, almost sad. "Things are different, outside of Villmark. And besides, we all know the people who leave never come back."

Oda and Arnóra murmured their agreement. Then the three of them sat quietly eating. It was almost like I could feel it, the memory they were sharing in that moment.

But Roarr caught my eye to give me a significant look, and I just gave him the smallest of nods.

Because we knew something these women didn't know.

We knew that people who left Villmark? Sometimes they did come back.

CHAPTER TWENTY

Roarr, Esja and I left Arnóra's house as quickly as we could politely make our exit. Roarr and I both immediately headed back to the main road and then south. Our steps were so hurried we were practically jogging, and a confused Esja trailed along behind us.

"Where are we going?" she asked. "You both seem to have come to the same conclusion, but I wish someone would clue me in."

"It might be nothing," I told her, but didn't slow down my pace at all.

"If Riki came back, he wouldn't be here. He'd be in the hamlet in the woods," Roarr said. "We can't get there, not with that wall in the way. But Haraldr checks in there all the time. He'll know if Riki is there or not."

"What about a hamlet in the woods?" Esja asked.

"There's a collection of cabins west of my place," I said, which I knew was vague. But the hamlet was deliberately not easy to find. "People from Villmark who go out to the wider world but then change their minds and want to come back, they stay there. It's sort of a mini-Villmark."

"But why can't they just come back?" Esja asked.

"These days? I don't even know," I admitted. "Villmark may be secret from the greater world, but the reverse has never been true. But the council decades ago made a decision, and that decision still stands."

"Some of the people who live there aren't entirely stable," Roarr said. "Not all of them. But some of them. Their experiences in the greater world, or maybe what drove them there in the first place, it makes them… well, unstable."

"And some," I felt compelled to put in, "just want to live with a foot in each world."

"But isn't that possible here?" Esja asked. "You do it."

"This might not be the time to press for reintegration," Roarr said.

"What, because of the ice wall between us and everyone else?" she asked.

"No, because of the isolationists," Roarr said. "They hate the greater world. People trying to live in both, they are going to hate that even more. It could create conflict."

"Maybe a necessary conflict," Esja said. "They need to learn how to adapt."

I didn't quite stumble in my half-jog, but I did look over at her a little longer than was safe when moving at such a speed. She saw my eyes on her and scoffed.

"I know what you're thinking. And yes, I'm friendly with a lot of them. I understand a lot of what they're feeling. That doesn't change what I said. They *do* need to learn how to live side by side with people who don't agree with them about everything."

"You should go to the council and ask them to revisit the old standing," Roarr said to her.

"I *should* go to the council," she agreed.

We had reached Haraldr's front door, but even though it was barely past dawn now, I was sure he'd be up. He woke with the birds. Still, I knocked as softly as I could, just in case.

I heard the shuffling sound of footsteps approaching the door. His live-in helper Fulla usually greeted guests, but I wasn't entirely surprised to see Haraldr himself standing there when the door swung open.

And he didn't look surprised to see me either.

"I was just about to sit down to breakfast," he said, gesturing for all three of us to come in. "Nothing fancy, just some crispbread and cheese and fruit. But there's more than enough to go around if you'd like to join me."

Not having even touched any of the cinnamon rolls at Arnóra's house, I was starving. And as much as what I really wanted was eggs and some sort of breakfast meat, crispbread with cheese and fruit was a good second option.

"We'd appreciate it," I said as I slipped out of my boots before stepping out of the entryway and up to his main corridor. "We've been up all night."

"Then it's a good thing I also have coffee," he said, then led the way down the corridor to his east-facing kitchen. The sun hadn't quite reached over the top of the ice wall yet, but the expanses of windows were letting in every bit of the morning light there was so far. Fulla was already there. Two places were set at the table, but she was pulling extra plates from the cupboard even as we came into the room.

"Coffee all around?" she asked.

"Yes, thank you," I said. She smiled at me before spinning back around to fetch more mugs.

"I gather this isn't about your rune," Haraldr said as he settled into his chair and pulled his own plate of already assembled food a bit closer. He cast an eye at Roarr, then at Esja, but said nothing more.

"We were wondering how long it's been since you were in the hamlet in the woods," I said.

"Oh, my," Haraldr said. He finished chewing a mouthful of crispbread and soft white cheese, a hand in front of his mouth as if half in thought and half in covering his chewing from view. Then he took a sip of coffee. "Obviously, it was before the wall appeared." He took another sip, still thinking. Then he wiped at his mouth before saying, "It was the day before we heard the petitions. Just a few days ago, then. Why?"

"We're wondering if someone new is in residence there," I said. "A man named Riki? About thirty-five or forty?"

"Oh, you know Riki?" Haraldr said, eyes widening in surprise.

"Only by reputation," I admitted.

"My mother used to sing me one of his songs, apparently," Roarr said.

"Yes, he was quite the sensation around town before he decided to leave," Haraldr said. "Nothing too lyrically complex in his songs, but the tunes were certainly catchy."

"Is he living in the hamlet now?" I asked.

Haraldr sat back in his chair and crossed his arms, as if this matter had taken a turn so serious he could no longer carry on eating.

"What?" I asked.

"I'm guessing these are not idle questions you're asking me right now," he said.

"I'm afraid not," I said.

"Do you think he's the reason for this ice wall around us?" Haraldr asked. He sounded like he was struggling to keep an open mind, but was losing that battle to his strong skepticism.

"No, unless you have some reason to think he has access to that kind of power?" I said.

"No, I doubt that very much," Haraldr said. "Then this is about the three men you've found inside the wall."

"I think he might be involved," I said. "He knew each of their wives rather well before he left town."

"He knew lots of young women rather well before he left," Haraldr said with a sniff of disapproval.

"Well," I said. "He's the only lead I have. Because their business connection doesn't seem to be the motive here."

"You think Riki killed these men?" Haraldr asked.

"I'd like to ask him some questions about it," I said.

"Well, you are correct. He is staying in the hamlet. He came back from the outside world about a month ago," Haraldr said.

"But?" I said. Because I could feel one coming.

"How are we going to ask him questions? There's a wall of ice between Villmark and that hamlet," Roarr guessed. "We knew that before we came. But I think we just wanted confirmation that he's here. Which he is. Kind of."

"How is he attacking these men from the far side of the wall?" Esja asked.

"Maybe he isn't on the far side of the wall," Roarr said.

"Valki and the patrols have done three thorough censuses of all of Villmark," Esja said. "We know who's here. And his name isn't on any list."

"And it's not like he could use a fake name," I added. "This is too small of a community for that to work."

"If he's killing these men, he must be here," Roarr persisted. "Somewhere."

"Are you certain he's your man?" Haraldr asked.

"No," I admitted. "I just want to talk to him. Which isn't possible. But knowing he's here, it would be a heck of a coincidence if he wasn't involved. He blows back into town, and then three of his old rivals mysteriously die? No, too big of a coincidence."

"There's more to it than that," Haraldr said with a sigh. "He's been a problem."

"What? Now or back in the day?" I asked.

He sighed even more heavily. "Both?"

"How so?" Roarr asked.

"When he left Villmark, it was as much to flee the consequences of his own actions as it was to…" He trailed off uncertainly.

"Find his fortune?" Esja suggested.

"Yes. Find his fortune," Haraldr said with a sparkle to his eye. "Just how he would describe it."

"What was he fleeing?" I asked.

"Not a crime, certainly," Haraldr said. "Just social consequences. He had chased too many young women, made too many promises. Angered too many young men. Things were about to reach a boiling point. I was new on the council at that point, but I can tell you, none of us were sorry to see the back of him. There was some lamentation from the women, but after a few months, we were well and truly shut of him."

"And now?" I asked.

"Now, Frór has been staying in the hamlet without taking a patrol assignment since Riki came back to town. Frór had to all but sit on him to keep him from charging into town the day he was back."

"I didn't even know Frór was back in town," I said with a familiar pang in my heart. Because Frór patrolled further out even than the Thors did. If anyone might possibly have had word of Thorbjorn and Loke, it was Frór.

If he hadn't come to see me, it must have been because he had nothing to report. Still. It wasn't like him. He always stopped in to see me when he was home, however briefly, and however sparse his news was.

"Your cat brought him back early," Haraldr said with a wry twist to his mouth. "It's almost like your cat knew that Frór would be needed before Riki even approached any of us about coming back."

"Yeah, that sounds like Mjolner," I said, and felt another pang in my heart. Wherever my cat was now, it was because he was needed where he was. But I didn't miss him any the less for knowing that.

"At first, Riki seemed to accept the rules. He settled into one of the cabins, and joined the gatherings of the other people in the hamlet. He even agreed to talk with Signi about what had happened out in the greater world and about his adjustment to life in the hamlet," Haraldr said.

Signi was one of the most prominent people in the hamlet. Born in Villmark, she had left to go to college in Duluth, to study psychiatry, of all things. She had gotten a master's degree, then a doctorate, then worked as a psychiatrist in Duluth for decades. She hadn't come home until she had gone into retirement.

Or semiretirement, anyway. In addition to helping other returning Villmarkers adjust, she also took care of the few people in Villmark who weren't mentally well enough to live among the rest of us. Like young Bera, who had pushed a woman into a well and killed her and had nearly killed me, all to win the love of a very uninterested Roarr.

And like Leifr, who had left Villmark as a young boy not for the wider world but for the magical realms that lay between Villmark and Old Norway. His was perhaps the most extreme case. He had spent untold lost years bouncing between magical realities. Repairing his mind was a long-term project for Signi, but one she was determined to succeed at.

She also still worked in the greater world, though. Mostly writing articles to professional publications and carrying on a correspondence with her peers. But when I said some people stood between the two worlds, she was who I thought of even before I thought of myself.

"Then what happened?" Roarr asked.

"He started slipping away from the hamlet. Not just wandering away distractedly. He was sneaking out, deliberately trying not to be seen by the others," Haraldr said.

"When you were there last, was he still there?" I asked.

"Yes," Haraldr said. "I was there specifically to speak with him, at Frór's request. Not that my admonishment did him any good. He hasn't changed much since he was fifteen. In one ear and out the other, as they say. But he certainly pretended to listen."

"That was the day before we heard the petitions," I said. "A night and a day before the wall went up."

"About thirty hours before the wall went up," Haraldr said. "Plenty of time for him to slip away again, although I think that's pretty unlikely."

"Why? You said he sneaked away, that implied he got outside of the hamlet at least once before," Roarr said.

"Four times," Haraldr said. "Each time he was caught by Frór and brought back to his cabin."

"So why is it unlikely he did it again?" I asked.

"Because Frór said he was going to chain that man to the central post in his cabin," Haraldr said. "He said it like a joke, I'll admit that. But I saw it in his eyes. He wasn't joking. Riki had pushed him too far."

Roarr's eyes widened in silent sympathy for whatever this Riki fellow was going through now. But it's not like anyone could say he hadn't had it coming. Knowing Frór, he had given many warnings beforehand.

"Why didn't he just get moved to one of the caves behind the waterfall?" I asked.

"Those are only for the most dangerous sorts," Haraldr said. "But if what you fear is true, if he really killed those three men, then that will surely be his fate."

"We have to find him first," Roarr said.

"We will," I said.

And I meant it. If I had to go room by room through every house in Villmark to find him, I would.

Because I knew he was here, inside the wall of ice. I felt it in my bones. He was here.

And he was probably watching us failing to stop him from killing again and again. But when I was done, I knew he wouldn't be laughing.

There were plenty of cozy little caves behind the waterfall, just waiting for him to move in.

CHAPTER TWENTY-ONE

AFTER LEAVING HARALDR, we headed due north, to Valki's house. It stood at the highest point in Villmark, just under the branches of the great tree. Which was also one of the places where Roarr had been setting up his markers.

But none of us needed to check his markers to know the wall of ice was definitely advancing. It was nearly to the trunk of the tree now.

"Is it moving faster?" Esja asked with a worried furrow to her brow.

"Is it?" I asked Roarr.

"Assuming my math is correct, it's gaining basically the same amount of ice every night. It's just each consecutive inward circle is smaller than the last, so the thickness of the new growth increases as the diameter remaining inside the circle decreases," Roarr said.

"If you say so," Esja said.

It wasn't exactly surprising that Esja—who had spent her entire life confined to her house south of Villmark even when she could get out of her sickbed—didn't have a strong grasp of math. She could read, and she had a real gift for art. But that was largely because her brother Loke had been diligent in bringing her stacks of books as well as all the art supplies she could ever want. After losing their parents at such a young age, he had done everything he could to keep Esja healthy and happy.

Honestly, math skills probably hadn't come up in either category. And so it was a lack in her education.

But there was something in the determined line to her forehead that told me the little careless shrug she had just given Roarr was just a show. She was going to pick a moment, probably after the wall came down but not too long after, to drop a seemingly idle comment about whether I could recommend a good basic math text for her.

Not that I had any idea where she should start. But now that I had noted that need to master a new topic furrowing her brow, I had a little time to prepare.

But for the moment, I had a different distraction for her. "Esja, do you still feel that feeling over at that part of the wall?"

"Oh, sure," she said, even though we were not particularly near the wall.

"From here?" I asked.

"Yeah. It's getting stronger," she said. "Maybe that's good news?"

"I feel like someone should be watching it, good news or bad," Roarr said.

"Yes," I said, but in a slow drawl.

I was planning to ask Valki to start a door-to-door search for any sign of Riki, and to ask everyone in Villmark if they'd seen him about or even just heard snatches of his songs. That was going to take a lot of people-power. But as we approached his front gate, which stood open to give us a full view of his front garden, I realized he was in the middle of different plans of his own.

It looked like he had had his patrol gather every brazier in the entirety of Villmark and bring them to his house. And then he'd set anyone remotely handy with tools to building more of them out of whatever makeshift bits of metal would suit. There were dozens and dozens of them all over his tiled patio.

"What's all this?" I asked as Roarr, Esja and I stepped into the garden.

"We're going to put them around the wall," Thorge told me as he straightened up from where he had been inspecting the bottom of one of the cruder makeshift braziers. "If we can get them hot enough, maybe we can hold the ice at bay."

So we weren't the only ones watching the growing encroachment of the ice. The whole town probably knew about it now. There was no way to get this many braziers together without alerting the entire populace. And there were only so many reasons they could be needed.

"You don't think this is going to make people nervous?" I asked.

"They're already nervous," Thorge said. "Not seeing us doing anything about it is what will lead to panic."

"I suppose," I said, unconvinced.

But it was Roarr who pointed out, "Just how much fuel do we have inside the town? Enough to burn all these day and night? For how long?"

"It's never going to be hot enough," Esja added. "The ice is too thick. But you already know that."

Thorge rubbed at his own shoulder as if in memory of the many hammer blows he had already delivered to that wall without the smallest effect. But he just nodded.

"I hear you. I do. But what else is there to do? Just wait? I'm not good at that," he said. "My wife is out there."

"She's with Nilda. I'm sure she's fine," I tried to assure him, but he was already shaking his head at me.

"You don't understand. We haven't told anyone yet besides our parents and Nilda, but she's pregnant," he said.

"Oh. Congratulations," Esja said. But she sounded confused, and who could blame her. Thorge's tone when he spoke those words was deadly serious, and I just knew that all the color had drained out of my face. I certainly felt like I needed to sit down. And judging from the sudden appearance of Roarr's hand at my elbow, it had to have been obvious I was having a strong reaction.

"It's early yet," I said to Thorge. "The problems with the women in her family started later in the gestational period. Didn't they?"

"I don't want to wait to find out," he said with a glower.

"No, of course not," I rushed to say. "I'm doing all I can."

"I know you are," he said, and put a comforting hand on my shoulder. But it dropped away almost at once. Like he only had that much to give. Not that I could blame him. In his shoes, I'd be going crazy.

"We think we know who killed Dufnall, Tunni and Litr," Roarr told him. I thought as much to distract him from thoughts of Kara and his coming baby as anything else. It certainly had that effect, as Thorge perked up at once.

"Do you, now?" he said, and gestured for one of the other men in the garden to go fetch his father. "Who is it?"

"It's a man named Riki," I said. "He left Villmark something like fifteen years ago. He's been living in the hamlet with the other returnees for about a month."

"I know who you speak of," Thorge said, the dark edge back in his voice. "Frór has kept my brothers and father and me up to date on him. He was being a problem. But how could he kill them with the wall between him and those men?"

"That's just it. We think he's hiding in town," I said.

"We've been keeping records of who's here since the first day the wall appeared," Thorge said. "We've got a count of everyone in town, every single name."

"He's hiding," Roarr said. "It's not like anyone has made a thorough search. The names on your lists are self-reported. Right?"

"Right," Thorge said. Then he held up a single finger, commanding the three of us to stay where we were as he turned to catch his father just coming out of the front door of the house. They spoke together in whispers while we awkwardly waited.

"Did you want to join the search?" Roarr asked me.

"For Riki? I don't think I'll be much help," I said. And not just because I was bone tired. "Honestly, I think I need to direct more of my attention to that spot in the wall. If Esja is feeling it more strongly, I need to try harder to sense it myself."

"I promise it's there," Esja said earnestly.

"Oh, I believe you," I said. "I just wish Mjolner was here. He helps me with this sort of thing. Without him, I feel like I'm half-blind. Magically speaking."

"Ingrid, well met," Valki said as he and Thorge both approached us. "Thorge tells me Riki is hiding inside Villmark. Any idea where?"

"No," I admitted. "Someone's basement or attic or backyard shed? I don't really know where to start."

"I do," he said with a twisted scowl. "With his mother. He was an only child, and his father passed a few years ago. But his mother still lives in town, not far from the marketplace. I'll call on her myself."

"I'll go with you," Thorge said, but his father was already shaking his head at him.

"No, I need you to direct the others in placing these braziers around the perimeter," he said. "I want everyone in Villmark to see them lit well before sunset."

"I don't think that's going to work," I said. "Nothing so far has even scratched this ice. I don't see it melting. Not unless the weather turns in our favor."

"No, it's too small a fire against too much ice," he agreed. "But we do what we can."

"It's a rallying symbol," Esja said. "There's magic in this ice. Mundane fire won't be able to fight it, but the fire in our minds and souls just might. We should have everyone who's willing gather around the fires."

"I don't think we'd even have to order that done," Valki said. "The people will be called to stand up. We'll bring this wall down, one way or another."

"But we're taking care of Riki first?" I asked.

"I'll deal with it," Valki said. "I know his mother a little. Enough to know she won't lie to me."

"Well, she might not know he's there," I said.

"Once I tell her what's been happening, she will be our ally in finding him," Valki said. "But I wanted to ask you. People keep talking about hearing singing. I've not paid enough attention to the rumors. I thought it was women's voices people were hearing. Something beyond the wall calling out to some of the men in Villmark. But now that I know it's Riki you're after, I'm not so sure."

"I don't think the music has been luring people out," I said. "Not even his music. Which, I gather, wasn't really siren songs."

"No. They were more hand-clapping, foot-stomping repetitive circles of songs," Valki said with the air of someone who was clearly not a fan. "But since Thorge here just said his name to me, I'm realizing I've been hearing those songs again lately. People in the streets have been whistling or humming bits of them. It's been happening since before the wall appeared, I'm sure of it."

"I gather the songs are real ear worms," I said. "They've been spreading around town like a virus. But a low-key one. Roarr was singing one, and he didn't even know what it was. Just a memory from his childhood."

"You're saying the music is literally infectious?" Valki said with a skeptical arch to his eyebrow.

"I think someone who encountered Riki, someone like you and your sons when you spoke to Frór about him or maybe even Haraldr, seeing him brought back memories of his songs," I said. "And one of you came back to Villmark, not telling anyone you'd seen or heard from Riki since that's against the rules, but quite unknowingly started humming or whistling or even singing one of his old songs. And someone else heard it and picked up the ear worm. They surely didn't even think anything of it, but later they'd repeat that song. Or maybe it triggered a memory of a different Riki song. Or of all his songs. Soon all of Villmark have heard snatches of these old half-forgotten melodies, and half of Villmark is still humming or singing them."

"No one knows Riki is here, because for most of the people of Villmark, the idea that anyone who leaves ever comes back is unthinkable," Roarr said. "And yet, his presence is everywhere. I honestly don't know where I heard anything that made me think of that song my mother used to sing. And yet there I was, singing it while I was setting out a platter of rolls." He ended with a shrug.

"He's infected the whole town," Valki said. Disdainfully, but not disbelievingly.

"That's not his actual crime," I felt compelled to point out.

"Surely not," Valki said. "I'll go see his mother at once. Are you coming with me?"

I was about to say yes, since this was a directed activity and not a random door-to-door search.

But what came out of my mouth instead was, "No. I have something else to attend to."

Valki raised that single eyebrow again, but didn't argue.

"I'll go," Roarr volunteered. Then he threw a look at me like he was asking my permission. "I think you'll only need Esja, really. For what you're going to do."

"For what I'm going to *try*," I clarified. "But yes. Thank you, Roarr."

He flushed a little, but gave me a quick nod before he and Valki strode out of the open gate.

"And just what are we doing?" Esja asked. I could tell she had wanted to go with Valki and Roarr. The idea of being there when Riki was caught and put in custody was tempting to her. Not that I blamed her. In other circumstances, I would want to be there too.

"We're going to get to the bottom of your happy feelings," I said. "I'm not sleeping again until this wall comes down."

She gave me an almost manic smile, then led the way back to that spot on the wall of ice that looked just the same as any other part.

One way or another, I was going to find out what was different about this spot.

CHAPTER TWENTY-TWO

Esja and I worked together all day, trying to figure out what made that particular section of the ice wall different from all the others.

No matter how much she tried to explain what she was sensing, I couldn't feel it myself. I tried meditating, but the frozen ground was far too uncomfortable for that to really work.

Then Thoralv had his assigned patrol set up a tent for us. It wasn't up against the wall like the ones blocking the murder victims from the view of others, but it was three-sided, with the tarp on the side facing the wall tied up and out of the way. Thick furs were layered on the ground inside the tent, and a kerosene space heater was placed inside, keeping the whole interior warm despite the open wall.

That was certainly more comfortable. But as it turned out, being more comfortable didn't help my meditation at all. Unless you considered sneaking an inadvertent nap a help. But when Esja poked me back awake, I didn't think it was.

All I had dreamed in those few moments of slumber was the sound of approaching skis. But they were still too far away to know who was coming on those skis. It was maddening.

I tried drawing some more. Then I tried scratching at the wall with my bronze wand. Which really wasn't how a magic wand was supposed to be used, but I was running out of options.

It didn't make a mark.

Thoralv came back just before sunset to deliver a basket of food to us, a nice picnic of roasted chicken and baked fingerling potatoes with apple hand pies for dessert.

"You must be worried too," I said to Thoralv. "Your alv girlfriend is on the other side of the wall too, isn't she?"

"Yes," he said. But there was a deeper sorrow on his face than I had expected to see.

"What is it?" I asked him.

"She's not the sort of alv that has a lot of magic," he said by way of preamble. "But usually, when we're apart, she sends dreams to me."

He flushed a little at that, and I decided not to ask what those dreams were about. Especially since I was pretty sure I knew why he was mentioning this now.

"You've not had a dream of her since the wall went up," I guessed.

"No," he said. "Sometimes when I'm not quite awake but not really asleep either, I feel like I can hear her calling my name. But I'm probably just imagining it. Longing for it."

"Sure," I said. "Or, she's trying really hard to reach you and not even this wall can keep her out entirely."

He perked up a little at that, but bit down on his lip as if forcing himself to quell that optimism before it took root. "I have to start checking all the braziers around Villmark. Do you need anything else before I go?"

"No, we're all set. Thanks," I said.

He nodded a farewell at me and then Esja and ducked out of the open wall of the tent. Leaving the two of us to stare at that expanse of blue ice once more.

"Do you dream?" Esja asked me. "I mean, of Thorbjorn. Or, like, my brother."

Her words came out in fluttering bursts, and I knew how much it had cost her even to ask. Because she was so sure the answer would hurt her when I said no.

I took my time chewing my mouthful of apple pie before swallowing to answer. "I keep dreaming of skis. Two people, I think, on skis. But I can't see them clearly, so I don't know who they are. And I'm not sure they're ever getting any closer."

Also, I had started dreaming of the skis the night before the ice wall had appeared. Were they even related?

I was so lost in puzzling that out that Esja's next words came to me like from the bottom of a deep well. "Do you think... maybe... that's Thorbjorn and my brother? Coming back? From far away, maybe?"

I closed my eyes and brought the few images that lingered in my memory from those dreams. "I mostly just hear the skis," I told her. "And I feel the cold, and I can smell the snow. But I've seen two figures at a distance. They're wearing long coats with the hoods pulled close around their faces."

"Okay," Esja said, the end of that word wavering between statement and question.

But I had to sigh. "I'm sorry, Esja. But I'm pretty sure the pair I'm seeing are a man and a woman. And I'm not sure if I know the man or not."

If I knew the woman, I couldn't imagine who she'd be. I'd met a few women who lived in the wilds north of Villmark, but I didn't see any reason for any of them to be heading my way now.

The one thing I was reasonably certain of was that it wasn't one of those golden-haired women who had been tormenting me and the people of Villmark since I had first arrived. The ones in league with Halldis. The ones who had once abducted all the Thors and Frór as well, keeping them locked in magic sleep inside a tower for weeks and weeks.

Magic sleep. That wasn't a welcome reminder. But their sleep had been unending, until the Mikkelsens and I had arrived to break that spell.

Was it related to what had kept us all sleeping when the wall appeared? I didn't think so. It just felt different. Not just because it was temporary. The Thors had been caught in tortuous nightmares when they had slept that magical sleep. But no one in Villmark had reported anything like that. I got the impression that most, like me, had woken early but refreshed, like after a restful night's sleep.

But anyway, the figure on the skis was wearing bulky layers of winter gear. And she was working hard, racing on those skis. That was two things I had never seen the golden-haired women do. They preferred curve-hugging, skin-revealing silken garments. And I couldn't imagine them ever doing anything so crass as working up a sweat.

"Ingrid?" Esja said, and I realized I had been quietly ruminating for some time. Quietly, but knowing me with a lot of expressions dancing across my face.

I would make a terrible poker player.

"This wall is a problem," I said, thinking out loud. "But it doesn't feel *evil*, does it?"

"No," Esja said in a slow drawl. "Even aside from this spot—which is getting stronger, by the way—it feels more like a too smothering hug than something trying to do harm. Do you think it was trying to protect us from Riki?"

"No, Riki is too small a thing for this to be about him," I said. "I mean, he's a monster who stalked and killed three men. But he's a mundane kind of monster. This is... something else."

"Loke said something was coming," Esja said.

Although I knew for a fact he had never said those words to her. She only knew about what he had been sensing because I had told her. But it was true. He and I had both felt it. A darkness was building power, and it was coming for Villmark.

"But this wall isn't a part of it," I said to myself.

We both jumped at a rustle of tent canvas, but it was just Roarr ducking inside. He flushed when he saw he had startled us both.

"Sorry," he said.

"No worries. We were just... caught up in a moment," I said. "We have chicken and potatoes here if you're hungry."

"Lovely," Roarr said, and flopped down on the furs between the two of us to dig into the basket. "It's all done," he said as he filled up a plate with meat and root vegetables. "Riki was hiding in his mother's basement, and she never knew. But he's in custody now. Not that we can get to the caves to put him where he belongs. But he's under guard in the council hall for now."

"He didn't put up a fight?" Esja asked.

"Nope," Roarr said and bit in to the drumstick we had left for him. He chewed for a moment, swallowed, then said, "He looked weird."

"Define 'weird'," I said.

"His color was weird. His skin was this dark color…" he trailed off, then looked at the drumstick in his hand. "Like this chicken. Like he'd been roasted to golden perfection. Until his skin crackled. Seriously, he looks way more aged than any of the men he killed. And they were all about the same age, right?"

"Sounds like he was hitting the tanning beds," I guessed.

"His hair was super light, too. Like more white than blond. But dry like straw," Roarr said. "And I thought he'd be taller."

"You're not exactly short," Esja pointed out before I could say the same thing.

Roarr flushed, but his brows were drawn down in confusion. Like he thought it might be a compliment she was giving him, but he wasn't sure. "I didn't mean taller than *me*."

"So he confessed right away?" I asked.

"Not right away," Roarr said. "At first he wanted to deny it. I mean, he wasn't supposed to be in town. And his mother was very angry that he'd been under her nose for days and days. Although frankly, I think she was just as mad she hadn't noticed as she was that he hadn't told her he was back."

"I'm sure there were enough things for her to be angry at to go around," I said.

"Yeah, so, at first he 'confessed' to being in town when he wasn't supposed to be. Made a big show of it. But Valki, of course, wasn't impressed. And then I was digging around in the room he'd been hiding out in, and I found three sets of clothes. Clearly not his. Again, I thought he'd be *taller*," Roarr said, as if to stress the fact that this hadn't been some vanity on his part, this thought.

"The missing clothes," I said. "Did the widows identify their husbands' things?"

"They didn't have to," Roarr said. "Once I showed them to Valki, I didn't even have to say a word. Riki saw I had them, and he broke down at once. I mean *broke down*, like in tears. It was... awful."

"I bet Valki hated it," Esja said.

"Yeah," Roarr said, as if the memory still haunted him. "To put it mildly."

"So that's that," I said, dusting the last of the bits of pie crust from my hands. "And yet the wall remains."

"We can't burn those braziers for long," Roarr said, although all three of us already knew this fact well. "Not even if people start sacrificing their furniture. Or their houses."

"We're not going to let it get to that," I said.

"Of course not," Roarr said at once.

If there was any way I could've thanked him for not pressing me for details, I would have. But that would've involved admitting that I didn't know how I was going to achieve that goal. Which would defeat the purpose of not going into details.

"So," Esja said, too loudly, as if she just had to break the tension of the moment. "How did he do it? How did he get them naked to the wall?"

"Oh," Roarr said. "I'm not entirely sure. He didn't explain. He just wept, and Valki gave up trying to ask him questions." Then he looked at me. "He was hoping you could talk to him at some point and clear up the details."

"Goody for me," I said glumly. I peeked into the basket, but the last apple pie was the one on the edge of Roarr's plate. Well, it wasn't like I needed another.

Esja drew up her knees and rested her chin on them, gazing sleepily at the wall through the open side of our tent. The only sound was a soft crackling from the braziers beside us and the even softer sound of Roarr eating fingerling potatoes one by one.

I didn't realize at first that I had fallen into another inadvertent nap. I don't even know exactly when it happened. I was just looking at that expanse of blue as the depth of color died with the setting of the sun behind the tent. And the crackling of the fire became a very different sound.

It morphed into the shush-shush of skis on snow.

The man and the woman were getting closer now, so close. So close if I squinted, I thought I might be able to see into the depths of their hoods. I saw eyes, eyes of a grayish-blue that echoed the ice I was still kind of staring into. I wasn't exactly asleep. But I was far from awake.

Then a sudden sound at my elbow had me jolting upright.

It was a meow.

More than that, it was Mjolner.

"Ah, your cat's back," Roarr said conversationally. Which told me volumes about how little he knew about my cat.

But before I could scoop Mjolner up and give him all the cuddles I had been dying to give him for days, the cuddles he would surely loudly object to, he slipped away from my side, heading straight for the ice wall in front of us.

"That's it," Esja said as she scrambled to her feet. "That spot he's heading for. It's the center of what I've been feeling."

I got up as well, and we lunged after Mjolner, who had reached the wall and was sitting there as prissily as ever.

He lifted a single six-toed paw and rested it on the ice. His toes were spread wide, and when he retracted the paw, they left a whitish patch like frost on the glassy surface of the ice.

"That's the spot," Esja said, little more than a whisper.

I'm not sure why, but we both leaned in close, so close our breath was in danger of frosting over the paw print.

Then I heard it. Faint, through what felt like an entire mountain of ice, but I knew I wasn't imagining it. But it wasn't skis I heard this time. It was the ringing of a hammer. Blow after blow of a hammer.

I looked up at Esja, and I knew as we shared a grin that she heard it, too.

"That's not just a hammer," I said to her. "And it's not just a hammer that's trying to get to us."

"It's a hammer that's *succeeding*," Esja said for me.

Mjolner just meowed, then headed over to Roarr, presumably to see how much chicken was left in that marvelous-smelling basket.

And the hammer kept on ringing. And, softer behind it, came the crunch of ice breaking.

CHAPTER TWENTY-THREE

THE NIGHT WAS ENDLESS, but there were no more naps for me, inadvertent or otherwise.

For the first hour or so, Esja and I stayed close by the wall, listening intently. But word spread around Villmark, and then there was too much noise around us for the ringing of the hammer to remain audible.

Which was okay. We knew it was coming.

And then it was joined by the ringing of other hammers, as Thorge and Thoralv both resumed pounding on the ice from our side of the wall. They traded blows over and over, like two members of a railroad crew pounding in stakes to the rhythm of a work song, only sideways.

It didn't take long for them to figure out that the ice was still impervious to even the mightiest of blows everywhere except for one tiny spot.

And Mjolner's paw print marked that spot.

More braziers were moved closer to light their work, and someone started hanging lanterns from the lower of the great tree's branches. I guessed that the perimeter of lit brazier fires plan was falling to pieces long before Valki made an appearance in the tent that was rapidly gaining a party atmosphere as we all waited in happy anticipation.

I tried a few drawings, but the energy around me was too upbeat for me to settle into a proper fugue state. Which was fine. Sometimes, even I would rather join a party. And when Ullr arrived with a hand-cart heavily loaded with kegs of ale, I gave up all together, putting my sketchbook away and letting someone put a mug of ale in my hands.

I wasn't much of an ale drinker. But I sipped at it as I pet Mjolner, who had finally resigned himself to my cuddles. Then he crawled into my lap and fell into a deep—and I was sure well-earned—sleep.

As the hours dragged on from midnight to the first hints of dawn, most of the party-goers dwindled away. A few curled up on the furs in the tent with the now-sleeping Roarr and Esja. But others wandered back to their homes, although I was sure they would all sleep as lightly as those in the tent.

Everyone was keeping their ears open for the sound of rescue coming in through the wall. No one wanted to miss it.

For my part, I couldn't take my eyes off that spot in the wall as it grew from a paw print on the ice to a divot, then to a hole in the wall, and finally into a tunnel barely large enough for a child to fit through. It was only just wide enough for the two Thors to keep swinging their hammers into the far end of it in an endless quest to get to the other side.

Roarr and I had contemplated how thick the wall must be now. Had it grown out even as it had grown in? Those layers would be thinner, as each successive circle in that direction would have *more* area to cover as it increased the diameter. So the rate of change in the thickness would be almost the opposite of what we were experiencing on the inside.

Roarr had kept at his numbers, trying to make some educated guesses at what the maximum thickness might be. But people kept refilling the mug of ale close by his hand, and I could see the effects of the alcohol glowing in his cheeks and glazing over his eyes long before he had given up and thrown down his pencil.

It didn't matter. Progress was being made. And no matter how thick the wall was, no one was going to stop tunneling through it until the job was done.

Finally, the sun rose from over the lake to the east. The sky, still cloud-free, grew rosy-pink long before we saw the sun as more than a slightly brighter point through the wall of ice. But something was different.

It was warm. At first I thought it was just because I was sitting so close to so many brightly burning braziers. But after I scrambled out of the tent to stand and stretch, I realized it wasn't just the stuffy interior of the tent that felt warm. It was everywhere.

I took off my hat and gloves. Then I unzipped my parka.

For their part, Thorge and Thoralv were already down to working in their shirt sleeves. And those shirts were drenched in sweat from their labors. But they weren't slowing. I didn't think either of them even could. Not so close to the end.

The sun was high enough to dance dazzling bright across the rim of the top of the wall, and it was too bright to look directly at. I shrugged out of my parka entirely, turning to set it inside the tent by my art bag.

And saw Mjolner looking up at me expectantly.

"What is it?" I asked him.

He gave me an abbreviated meow that sounded like a chirrup, then walked past me to where the Thors were pounding on the wall.

Then he meowed louder, more insistently. Thorge glanced down at him, but neither he nor his brother stopped what they were doing. They had a rhythm to maintain.

Mjolner meowed again, sounding annoyed. Then he looked back over his shoulder at me, his yellowish-green eyes almost accusing.

"Guys, I think he wants you to stop for a minute," I said. Which was half a lie. I was pretty sure Mjolner wanted them to quit, full stop. But as much as I doubted I could get them to take even a momentary break, I knew for sure I couldn't get them to put down the hammers all together.

"Drink some water," Roarr said as he brushed past me to bring a canteen to the brothers. So he was awake. I looked over my shoulder to see Esja sitting up and yawning, then frowning in confusion as she found herself pulling at the scarf wrapped warmly around her throat. Too warmly now.

"It's getting warmer," I told her. "Not summer warm, but October warm."

"Too warm for this," Esja said, tossing the scarf aside. "Why are we stopping?"

"Mjolner—" I started to say, then realized the cat was moving into the tunnel the Thors had burrowed into the wall. We all watched him explore that space, each of us making as little noise as possible. Thorge drank his fill, then handed the canteen to Thoralv without a word.

Mjolner made another chirruping little meow, like a question. Or like someone testing an echo.

I got down on my hands and knees and poked my head into the space behind him. Despite their efforts, the tunnel wasn't very deep. Mjolner could fit into it, but no one bigger than a small toddler was going to be able to manage it. So this wasn't our way out.

Yet.

Then Mjolner yelped in alarm and before I knew what was happening, I had a cat catapulting into my chest. He hit me hard enough to knock me back on my butt.

Knocking me clear of the wall just in time.

As I held a squirming Mjolner in my arms and tried to use just my elbow to get myself back up to sitting, I saw something happening at the far end of the truncated tunnel.

The ice was splitting. Quivering. Breaking free.

There was a flash of silver, like the corner of something just busting through to our side.

And, just like that, the entire wall came down. That hammer blow from the far side didn't just break through. It broke the whole spell.

There was a confused moment of ice cracking all around Villmark, then a sound like water rushing everywhere. But I couldn't see anything clearly. We were all encased in fog, although this wasn't a snowy, frozen fog. This fog was thick with moisture, like high humidity on a cold morning.

Not pleasant. It felt like it soaked through the thickness of my whole wool sweater in the blink of an eye.

But then a breeze picked up. A breeze from out over the lake, carrying with it all the smells of the shore of Lake Superior. A hint of fish, probably from the shacks down in Runde, a stronger smell of pine, all layered over the dry smell of dead autumn leaves.

The breeze swirled through the fog, then lifted and carried it away.

The ground underneath me was sopping wet, like if the heaviest of thunderstorms had been raging here for days on end. It was supersaturated and soaking through the seat of my jeans.

But I was completely incapable of moving, even to get to my feet and out of the icy cold water.

Because there was a figure emerging into view as the fog dissipated. I couldn't see the face, only the barest suggestions of a silhouette against the rising sun behind him. But I didn't need to see his face to know who he was. Just the outline as he stood there, breathing hard as he rested on the long handle of the immense hammer that was planted now between his feet, was enough.

A fiercer breeze blew over us, making all the lanterns in the tree dance, although their light was lost to the brighter light from the sun. But the last of the fog went with that breeze.

And I was looking up into the thickly bearded but warmly smiling face of Thorbjorn Valkisson.

He put out a hand to help me to my feet, but when I took it, he didn't just let me use him for support. He pulled me up with so much force I went past standing on my own two feet to collide into him.

Into his chest.

Into his embrace.

He did take a moment to whisper my name, so softly I don't think anyone around us could hear it. But my heart was beating so loudly in my ears in that moment, I have no idea what anyone else could hear.

And I really didn't care.

Because then he was kissing me, with all the pent-up emotions of our months apart.

And I was kissing him back with the same.

He was back. I finally had my Thorbjorn back.

CHAPTER TWENTY-FOUR

I COULD'VE STAYED that way forever. But I was all too aware that standing right behind me was a small crowd of people who also loved and had missed Thorbjorn. So I had to let him go. Although I knew he wasn't going far. Just from my arms to that of his father and two of his brothers. And I was sure someone had already sprinted to the Valkisson house to fetch his mother.

It was only after he had slipped away from my embrace that I could pay attention to anything else in the world at all. Like the fact that I was standing ankle-deep in icy water from the rapid melting of the wall.

Or that Thorbjorn hadn't been alone. Although the companion who had been standing behind him and was now throwing back their hood and loosening the fastenings on their parka wasn't Loke. It was a woman of indeterminate age, lanky and tall, like a professional basketball player. She had a quiver full of arrows strapped to one hip, and a long knife on the other.

I could see the ends of a bow strapped across her back, as well as a pair of skis with poles.

But even if that hadn't been hint enough, she met my gaze, and I recognized the gray-blue of her eyes at once. I had been dreaming of her approach.

"You brought Thorbjorn home to me," I said to her.

She gave a single nod even as she fussed with removing her gloves and stuffing them into the pockets of her fur-lined parka.

"Loke?" Esja asked in a small voice just at my elbow.

The woman said nothing, but there was a sudden firmness to the line of her mouth that surely meant something. But before I could press her, Nilda and Kara came up from behind her, picking their way through the shallower of the puddles. And behind them was my grandmother.

"Mormor!" I cried, and splashed over to her to pull her into a tight hug.

"I knew you were well," she said as she patted my back. But there was a catch to her voice that told me as much as she had wanted to believe that, she hadn't *known* it.

"Do you know what caused this?" I asked.

"Yes, but I'll let Thorbjorn explain it," she said.

"But what about my brother," Esja said, no longer in her small voice.

"Your brother remains in the north," Thorbjorn said as he came up from behind her to rest a hand on her shoulder. There was a puzzled frown on his face that grew to complete astonishment when Esja spun around to fix an icy glare on him. "Esja! You look... different."

"Never mind how I look," she snapped back. Most of the color on her cheeks was from anger, but I thought there was just a smidge that was a response to the implied compliment in the way he said *different*. "Where's my brother?"

"In the Ironwood, or at least he was the last I knew of him," Thorbjorn said.

"The Ironwood?" Roarr said. "Isn't that a place of monsters? Trolls and jotuner and the like. Not welcome to strangers. I mean, I thought not even Frór went near that place."

"That was his destination, for reasons he never shared with me,"

Thorbjorn said. "We parted ways at the edge of the forest. Because while I was not welcome there, apparently he was."

"He could be dead!" Esja said.

"No, I don't think he is," Thorbjorn said. He gripped both her arms in his hands, holding her tightly. She squirmed a little, but I had seen her make serious efforts to break free from someone's grasp, and what she was doing now wasn't that.

"You don't know. You left him," she said.

"I stayed at the edge of the wood for as long as I was able," he said in his warmest, kindest tone. "I waited so that we could return home together. But he never came out again. And then the weather turned, quite unexpectedly. I didn't have enough food to eat or fuel to burn to remain where I was. It simply wasn't safe for me to venture even a little ways into the shade of those trees. And where I was camped was bare tundra. Covered in snow with no game in sight? I couldn't stay."

"So you left him," Esja said.

"Loke always knew we would part ways," he said. "That had always been his plan."

Esja lapsed into sullen silence. Which left an opening for Roarr to ask, "Who's your friend?"

We all looked at the tall woman with the skis on her back. With her hood down and her parka open, we could see her long, pale blonde hair in its thin braids. She didn't have the golden tones of a Mikkelsen, and while I was sure she was all lean muscle, it wasn't the same as theirs. She didn't look like a valkyrie. Maybe she was some kind of hunter?

"This is Skadi," Thorbjorn said, moving from Esja to stand by the new woman's side. "She saved me after I had been trapped under snow from an avalanche for more than a day. And she brought me all the way home. I owe her more thanks than I can ever repay."

"It was on my way," Skadi said with a small but clearly dismissive hand gesture.

"What do you mean, on your way?" I asked. "You were coming to Villmark?"

"Not specifically," she said, and shifted from foot to foot. I got the profound sense that answering all these questions was pulling more words out of her than she usually spoke in a week. And she didn't like it. But she pressed on. "I was following the trail of a troop of jotuner who had come south out of the Ironwood. I wanted to know what they were up to. Knowing jotuner, it was surely no good."

"Jotuner," I said. "You mean giants?"

"Ice giants," Thorbjorn said. "They don't usually come down out of the north, and they certainly don't travel in troops. But something was compelling them. And they were moving fast. Skadi and I skied day and night, but it was impossible to catch up with them."

"They did this?" I asked, gesturing at the puddles all around us, meaning the ice wall.

"I believe so, yes," Thorbjorn said. "They were also responsible for the weather that drove me away from the Ironwood, and for the avalanche that washed over me in the middle of an alpine meadow wide enough where I should've been safe from such things."

"Why?" I asked.

"Which part?" he asked, brows furrowing.

"Any of it?" I said.

"Jotuner are agents of chaos. This is true," my grandmother said to all of us. "But most of that is unintentional chaos. They came south to build this wall, but by their very nature, they brought the chaotic, icy weather with them."

"It's warmer because they're gone now?" I asked.

"The hammer the hag gave us broke the spell of the cold air before we even got started at bringing down the wall," Thorbjorn said, and slapped the hammer that hung from his belt. It looked like it was crafted from liquid silver, almost like it was moving like ripples across a pond. Although I had seen it when it had broken through the ice. I knew it was quite solid.

"The hag?" was all I managed to say.

"The hag, like Skadi and I, was chasing after the ice giants. She spoke in riddles, but I'm sure she knew she would never catch up. That hadn't been what she was sent to do," Thorbjorn said.

"Where's this hag now?" I asked.

"Gone, like the giants," Nilda said. "Kara and I met her briefly, when she was still speaking with Thorbjorn and Skadi. But she made herself scarce when she saw Nora coming."

"She turned into an auk and flew away, heading due north," Kara said. I couldn't help beaming at her when I turned my attention to her. And I knew she knew why. I could tell by the way she touched one hand to her still-flat stomach. But now wasn't the time for congratulations. Or the more serious talk that would have to come after the congratulations.

"Was she afraid of you?" I asked my grandmother.

"She ought to be," my grandmother said, gripping her walking stick like she was about to brandish a weapon. But then she softened a little. "I don't think she knew who I was. She had delivered her gift and her message, such as it was. There was no more reason for her to stay. And her kind does not like to stray beyond the confines of the Ironwood."

"Did she send the giants, then?" I asked.

"I don't think so," my grandmother said. "No, I got the sense that whatever entity sent the jotuner later sent her, to bring the hammer as an apology for the chaos the jotuner brought in their wake."

"I should've written down what she said," Thorbjorn said regretfully. "But we'd only just reached Villmark and saw the wall. I hadn't even started to figure out a way inside when she just appeared there, standing with Skadi and me with this immense hammer in her hands."

"She didn't say all of it, whatever she was reciting," Skadi said. "The arrival of your friends interrupted her." She glanced from Thorbjorn to Kara and then to Nilda.

"We were patrolling the wall perimeter, like we've done every day and night since this wall appeared," Nilda said. "Stumbling on the two of you with the hag when we did was just happenstance."

My grandmother made a soft snort, but said nothing.

"And your arrival so soon after?" I asked her.

"Not happenstance," was all she said.

"So something out of the north sent a troop of giants—sorry, jotuner—to build a wall around Villmark, and then sent a hag with a gift to make up for it?" I said. "Who is behind it all, then? The golden-haired women?"

"I'd maybe think it's possible if only the jotuner were involved," Roarr said. "But the hag with the apology gift? That's not like them at all."

"The wall felt protective. Remember?" Esja said to me.

"Right," I said. "But, like, a smothering kind of protection. So whoever sent the jotuner to build it must've realized it was too much. Hence giving us the hammer to bring it all down again."

"Makes sense," Roarr said.

"Except I still don't get why anything up in the north would do this," I said. "Every time I've been up there, the only things interested in us have felt completely malevolent. That, or they're benign but ambivalent. But nothing is kindly interested in us. Not protective at all."

"I felt eyes on me," Thorbjorn said in a dark, quiet voice. "Things inside the Ironwood were watching me the entire time I camped just out of reach of the shadows of its trees. And on the way home again, even through the fiercest weather, I felt other eyes on me. I'm pretty sure it was the golden-haired women. Although they never made themselves known. And they disappeared entirely once Skadi joined me."

"But they didn't do all this," I said.

Although I was sure that they, like Riki, weren't above using the chaos in the ice giants' wake for their own sinister reasons.

The murders. I still had to tell Thorbjorn and my grandmother about the murders.

But my grandmother was looking at all of us with a bemused smile on her face for some reason.

"What?" I asked, feeling like someone who had accidentally gotten food on their face.

"None of you have guessed?" she said, even more amused.

"Wait, you know who did this?" I said. Where had I missed the obvious clue?

But my grandmother just tipped her head to Esja. Who was

looking too still, too pale. If she had figured out what my grandmother already knew, she found it far less amusing.

"Esja?" I said.

Esja sighed, a weary, annoyed sigh. Like she was just fighting the urge to roll her eyes in exasperation.

"It was my brother," she said. "Obviously. Who else would send a troop of jotuner to encase an entire village in a wall of ice just to keep me safe from something that wasn't even harming me?"

I opened and closed my mouth a few times, as arguments forming in my mind broke apart before I could quite utter them.

No, it all made sense. It was exactly the kind of thing Loke would do.

CHAPTER TWENTY-FIVE

ROARR HADN'T BEEN wrong about Riki looking weird. I supposed it was ironic. In pursuit of some goal of youthful looks, he had fake-baked and bleached himself into a look that, with just a few adjustments to his wardrobe, would best be described as geriatric beach bum. And he wasn't even that old. He just looked worn out.

And if that sounds mean, all I can say is that his looks were probably the most pleasant thing about him.

Because, a few days after the wall came down, I could no longer put off doing as Valki had asked and sitting down with Riki to get his story straight about what he had done. And so I had gone to see the former Villmarker in the cave where he was going to be kept for the rest of his life. It wasn't so deep as the cave that contained Halldis, but I'm not sure if he knew or cared about this fact.

He was pretty committed to feeling sorry for himself. Like three murders were just some mistake he had kept making over and over again.

Premeditated mistakes.

I found him very hard to take. Fortunately, I hadn't gone to see him alone. I had brought Roarr and Esja with me, hoping they would prompt me with any questions I forgot to ask.

And I also brought Thorbjorn. Who had been brought up to speed on everything that had happened, but was mostly just there for moral support. For me. Because I needed it.

"You do know I had nothing to do with it," Riki said for the zillionth time.

"Yes, we're well aware you had nothing to do with the appearance of the ice wall," Roarr said drily as I viciously bit my tongue and pretended to concentrate on my sketching. "Again, we never thought you did."

"You sure took advantage of it, though," Esja said. She was still a little unnerved by being the unwilling cause of yet another huge weather effect in Villmark. First, the spirits in her house brought a hailstorm down on all of us in an attempt to keep her trapped inside, then her brother sends giants to do pretty much the same thing.

But I think she was also blaming herself a little bit for Riki's three murders. Which I didn't think was fair of her.

"Riki," I said, pausing in my drawing to spin my pencil through my fingers for a moment. "You took advantage of the sudden appearance of the wall as your brilliant way to disappear the bodies."

Yeah, I was being sarcastic. I mean, every one of them had been seen right away. He might have gotten away with things a little longer if he'd dropped them down the well in the commons. Although in my town, no one gets away with murder. In the end, we always find them out.

"But the wall wasn't part of your original plan, was it?" I asked.

I tried to sound interested and eager. Please, genius serial killer man, tell me all about your superior planning skills.

Riki smirked, and I immediately set back to work sketching him. In dark, angry strokes. But I let him talk.

"No, you're right about that," he said. "At first, I even thought it would be a hindrance. I had intended to bring them outside of town, you see. But I couldn't do that with that wall in the way. So I had to improvise. I'm a planner by nature, you know. But I think I improvised pretty handily."

"Did you," I said flatly.

Thorbjorn stroked at his chin, as if missing the growth of beard he had trimmed away along with great lengths of his hair. He always did that, when he was home. Then it would all grow out again while he was out in the wilds.

Not that I minded his wild look. In fact, I kind of preferred it. Because when his hair was short and his beard was well kept, he always seemed to be missing it. He would run his fingers through his hair with a look of momentary wonder at where it had all gone. And he would stroke his chin like this.

And I knew he was more used to being away than being home. That was his normal, being out in the wilderness looking unkempt. Even if he didn't know it about himself.

But in this moment, he was stroking his chin as he regarded Riki with assessing eyes. Then he said, "I know Ingrid understands what happened, but can you walk me through the steps of your plan?"

"It was perfectly simple," Riki said, deepening his smirk. I kind of wanted to stab him with my pencil for condescending to my boyfriend. But I knew Thorbjorn had set him up to do this. To rattle off everything in a smug show, all at once. And I could draw the entire time, without interruption.

"Okay, but explain it to me," Thorbjorn said.

"Those men were responsible for driving me out of town all those years ago," Riki said.

Apparently, the idea that he had left to find his fortune had quite disappeared from his memory. But I didn't say a word. I just kept drawing.

"I made an honest effort to succeed out there in the greater world, but the odds were always stacked against me. It isn't my place, you know? I belong here," he said, gesturing at the ground beneath his feet.

Which was funny. It was almost like he was talking about his prison cell.

But he kept on talking. "They got rid of me because I was their competition. None of them would've ever ended up with their wives if I had stayed around, and they knew it."

Setting aside that no one in Villmark would've allowed him to have four wives, not least of all Ronnok, Oda, Arnóra and Njorun.

"After years away from my people, from my home, I come back to find I won't even be allowed back inside? Ever?" He shook his head with a chuckling scoff. "And they just get to carry on as if they have no responsibility for my fate? No. I'm sorry. I'm a Villmarker, born and bred. I can't stand for that. I can't let that attack on me and my family line stand. I was owed blood."

Thorbjorn chewed at his lip, and I could see him wrestling with the need to lecture this man on what being a Villmarker really meant. But he fought down that urge and just said, "Go on. How were you going to get that blood?"

"Obviously I couldn't call for a holmgang," Riki said, as if he too knew what Thorbjorn had been thinking.

"Because you have no weapons training to ever win in a duel?" Esja asked, sitting back with her arms crossed in a way I *knew* she knew made her increasingly sizable biceps pop.

"No," Riki said, flustered. "I mean, that's not why. But anyway, the four of them don't train with weapons either. They're all carpenters."

"But if you thought you could take them in a fair fight, why didn't you ask for a holmgang?" she persisted.

"Aside from no one doing that in decades, I wasn't even allowed inside the limits of Villmark," Riki said. "It's hard to challenge someone to anything when society has decided you don't actually exist. I was confined to that crummy little hamlet deep in the woods. How was I going to get word out? Carrier pigeon?"

"People move back and forth," Esja said. "You wouldn't need a pigeon to send a message."

"We're getting off topic here," Thorbjorn said.

"Oh, I don't know," Roarr said. "I'm finding it rather interesting that he couldn't challenge anyone to a holmgang because he wasn't allowed to enter Villmark, but he had no problems getting inside Vill-mark to murder three people."

"That was out of desperation," Riki said. "You all drove me to that. All of you!"

"Here's the thing," Thorbjorn said, leaning forward with his elbows on his knees. His hands were just dangling loosely. It was a deceptively casual posture. "You didn't actually kill anyone, did you?"

I watched a cascade of emotions wash over Riki's face. Confusion, suspicion, then something like elation.

"That's right. I didn't," he said. "I didn't kill anyone."

"Wait, what?" Roarr asked, looking from Riki to Thorbjorn and back again. I just kept on sketching. Because I knew where Thorbjorn was going with this.

"It's true," Thorbjorn said, sitting back in his chair to regard Roarr. "Riki here just invited these men over to his place for an ale. Just to have a chat and clear the air. And after they'd had that ale—I'm guessing just a single ale for each of them, as they were family men eager to get back home and not drink themselves silly with someone who really wasn't even an old friend, because let's be honest here—after they'd had that ale, Riki here just walked them out of his place. He had to help them along. They weren't in good shape. But as much as they were stumbling about, they were joyfully cooperative."

"Why?" Esja asked. "Why would they just go with him?"

"Because they were drugged," I put in, even as my hand kept sketching. "Like Arnóra and her children. But not with anything anyone in Villmark would recognize. Something modern. Something he brought with him from his time out in the greater world."

Roarr was frowning intently now. "Date rape drugs? Is that what you mean?"

"Sounds like it to me," I said.

Roarr turned his gaze to Riki, and the dark scowl on his face was enough to make me feel like cowering back. And it wasn't even directed at me.

"I, well, yes," Riki stammered. "That's what it was. And yes, Thorbjorn, well spotted. A single ale each." He was clearly trying to still sound like the smug genius serial killer bragging about his plan. But he was also starting to sense the room was turning against him. "That was all they would agree to, but it was all I needed. And they never suspected a thing."

"You drugged them," I said, turning a page and resuming my sketching without pause. "Then you stripped them down to their underpants. And then you left them out in the cold, sitting against a wall you knew would close in over them. And you just left them there to die."

"It was almost too good for them, really," Riki said, getting some of his old steam back. "They were euphoric. They felt warm and comfortable. And when I had set them down where I wanted them to die, they just let it happen. Honestly, I'm surprised none of them thanked me."

"You left them to die," Thorbjorn said. "Alone."

"I didn't need to hang around to watch," Riki said. "It was inevitable at that point. Plus, it was really cold out there."

"And you knew the ice wall would cover up their bodies," I added. Because I knew where Thorbjorn was driving this conversation.

"Yeah," Riki said. But he seemed to be detecting the trap closing in around him.

Too late, though. Way too late.

"You hid the bodies," Thorbjorn said, stressing each word.

And Riki blanched. He had finally figured it out.

"You said before I hadn't actually killed anyone," he rushed to point out. "That's still true. I didn't."

"But you left them to die," I said. "And as much as we could debate for days on whether that's the same thing or not, it's all academic. Because when you hid the bodies, you declared it a crime. It wasn't a moment of angry passion. And it certainly wasn't a duel. It was you eliminating men you thought of as rivals and hiding the evidence of what you had done."

"Which is not how we settle feuds in Villmark," Thorbjorn said with a fierce glower that had Riki recoiling in his chair.

"And you're very lucky that what you dosed those kids with didn't do them any long-term harm," I added.

Then I snapped my sketchbook shut. Because we were done here.

The four of us walked silently out of the cave, then up the long passage to the cavern and natural stone steps that led up to the meadow.

Where it was a sunny day. And the temperature was exactly as warm as it should be for late October.

"What we were talking about before?" Esja said to me. "About speaking to the council about changes? I think we still have to do that."

"What's this?" Thorbjorn asked.

"We were discussing the problems with how we reintegrate people who return to Villmark from the greater world," I said. "Or, rather, how we don't do that. But we should."

Thorbjorn frowned for a moment, but I could tell he was just trying to parse my rambling sentence. Because in the end he just nodded. "Yes. We should be as free to come and go from all the world as we are from Runde. Although I fear the council will take a very long time to come around to that."

"That's okay," Esja said brightly. "These days, I have the energy for a long fight."

Then she took off towards Villmark at a dead sprint. As if the other three of us had any doubts about her words.

CHAPTER TWENTY-SIX

THAT NIGHT, all of Villmark—or, at least, most of it—gathered in the village commons for a spontaneous bonfire. It wasn't any kind of holiday. It was just a crisp night after a warm day when the air still smelled of autumn leaves from the forests all around us, and who knew how many more of those we'd have before winter?

It was nice to sit by a bonfire that was just for fun and not a desperate means to protect all of us from danger.

And it was even nicer to enjoy that bonfire with Esja by my side, not trying to get closer to it. Not setting herself on fire.

It really felt like that phase of her life was over now.

From where the two of us were sitting, I could see Thorbjorn with Thorge and Thoralv. Judging from their body language, they were telling tales of what they'd each been up to in the last two months. And I was sure those tales were heavily embellished. And that their gestures would only grow larger as the night wore on and the ale kept flowing.

I didn't mind that he wasn't sitting with the two of us. I was just glad that we were only this far apart, where I could still see him and know he was well.

Esja, beside me, sighed. As if she had heard my thoughts, and they had made her miss her brother anew.

"Aren't you going to join the others in dancing?" I asked, pointing to where Skefill and Raggi were helping a band of traditional Nordic musicians set up. I didn't know the men in that band personally, but I had heard them perform on occasion in Aldis' mead hall. I knew they were talented. And that Esja enjoyed dancing to their rhythms a lot.

But Esja just shook her head. "No, I'm fine here with you. If you don't mind?"

"I never mind your company," I assured her.

Then we lapsed back into a companionable silence. The crackling of the bonfire didn't quite drown out the voices of the Villmarkers gathered around it, but it *was* loud. Like it was a living thing, one that was anxious it wasn't the center of attention it thought it should be.

"Ingrid? Can we talk about my brother?" Esja asked.

"Of course we can," I said. "Did you want to go back inside?" I looked back over my shoulder towards the front gate of my house.

But she was shaking her head. "No, no one is close enough to us to hear. Or cares enough to try to listen, anyway."

She sounded so sad. She was sitting with her knees drawn close to her chest, and as she talked, she rested her head on those knees, her face towards me.

"I know you miss him," I said.

"It's not about that," she said before I could go on. "It's about his magic."

"Oh. Well, I have to be honest with you. I don't really understand much about his magic," I said.

I barely understood my own magic.

"You know he's sort of at the mercy of it, right?" she said.

"That's part of why he went north," I reminded her. "To see if he could learn how to control it. But I think if he'd succeeded, he'd already be back here with you."

"I agree," she said. "But I've been thinking, and I don't think there's anything in the north that's going to help him."

"The more I hear about the north, the vaster it becomes in my mind," I said. "I guess what I'm saying is, anything is possible."

"I just mean… I think he needs to come home to master his power," she said.

"Okay. Why?" I asked.

"I think…" But she stopped talking, closing her eyes as if mentally reviewing something she had already practiced saying. Then she opened her eyes and looked intently at me before speaking. "You know he can't control where he goes, right? He opens one door and steps through some other door, maybe across town and maybe in some entirely different country."

"Sometimes he can control it," I said. "But, yes. I know what you mean. He feels like when he's taken somewhere he didn't intend to go, that there's some sort of reason for it. So he pokes around for a problem to solve before coming back home again. But, yes. His control is imperfect."

"Right. But that's about space, right?" she said.

"Space?" I repeated. For some reason, I thought she was talking about emotional space.

"But I think it's also about time," she said significantly, and I caught up with her meaning.

"Why do you think that?" I asked.

"Well, because of the wall," she said. "The timing of it doesn't make any sense. Unless Loke is in some place where time doesn't flow the same as it does here. And not just faster or slower. The difference isn't even uniform. It's random. Chaos."

"That's a lot to surmise about an ice wall appearing in October," I said.

"No, that's not the timing I'm talking about," she said. "Look, he sent the jotuner to build that wall because he thought it would protect me. But that wall was huge. So what could he possibly think he had to protect me from?"

"I don't know," I said. "Maybe something that isn't here yet. Is that what you mean?"

"No, I think it's about what's been happening to me," she said. "I mean, we still don't know what caused it. But three times I've set myself on fire. And that wasn't my decision. Something powerful was directing me."

"Something with enough magical power that having jotuner build an ice wall to keep it out maybe isn't total overkill," I said. "So you think he knew it was about to happen and sent the jotuner, but because his flow of time is so different from ours, he was super late in giving the order."

"But then the hag came, so much closer to the right time with the hammer to make up for it," Esja said. "Doesn't it make sense?"

"I promise you, nothing about time travel ever makes any sense to me," I said. "But it's a sound theory. It explains our observations. I just don't know how we would test it."

Esja nodded, then turned her head to watch the flames dancing in the center of the commons. I waited for her to gather her thoughts, because I could tell she had more to say to me.

"Loke is unanchored from everything," she said at last, in little more than a whisper. "He can't find a fixed point in space or in time. And I don't think he's going to be able to fix that in the north. Because I think I'm the anchor he needs."

I bit at my lip, thinking her words might be a little too true. Because as long as I had known Loke, he had considered his sister and her wellbeing his lodestone. All of his life revolved around that. Or it always had, until he had gone to the north.

"I don't mean I'm a drag or a responsibility weighing him down," Esja said with eerie prescience. "I mean, after what I've just gone through, I'm a fixed point."

"We don't know for a fact what happened to you was about the Norns—" I started to say.

But she held up a hand to belay my words. "Ingrid, please. I think we know. Maybe not in facts, but in our bones. We can feel it. Both of us. I was possessed by the past, then by the future, and finally, now, by the present. And I'm still there, in the present. That's where this entire experience has left me. I can see the influence of the past all around us, and I get a sense of how that's going to be expressed in the future.

But I've never felt more like this moment that I'm in is, in all ways that matter, where I actually live. And I realize that is probably ironic, since I was bedridden for so long that the passage of time was kind of an obsession for me for years."

"You feel different from before?" I asked.

"Well," she said, and moved just enough for me to become aware all over again of just how heavily muscled her entire frame was these days.

"I didn't mean physically," I said. "You feel like you live in the moment?"

"Not like that," she said, rolling her eyes. "I've read enough modern fiction to know what that means. That's a lifestyle choice, or whatever. What I'm talking about is how I perceive things. Like they used to be in black-and-white, and now everything is in full living color. It's just part of who I am now. And I don't feel like that's going to change. The process I've been going through, I think it's complete."

"And?" I prompted.

"I feel good," she said, leaning over to bump my shoulder with her own.

"But you still miss your brother," I said.

"More than that. I need to be with him," she said.

"Please tell me you're not planning to go after him," I said desperately. "I just got Thorbjorn back. I don't want to lose you now."

"That's sweet," she said. "But no. I don't think going to find him would work out."

"Because he's chaos and you're a fixed point?" I asked.

"Something like that," she said with a half smile. "Mostly, he's got to come to me. I was just hoping, maybe, I could borrow your cat? To send him a message."

"Absolutely," I said, relieved to find that her plan was actually a sensible one. "Mjolner would be honored, I'm sure. Although I don't think he's out here now for the party."

I started to look around, but Esja grabbed hold of my arm, like she was afraid I was about to get up.

"I don't have it ready yet. I need a little time to figure out what I want to say," she said. "Be honest, what I just said to you was pretty garbled."

"I think *you* know what you mean," I said, as diplomatically as I could.

She just laughed. "Yes. I definitely need a little time to get the wording right. But when I'm ready, I can borrow Mjolner?"

Before I could answer, there was a meow that came from directly between us. And I looked down to see my six-toed black cat squirming into the tight space between my hip and Esja's. He blinked up at me, then shifted to make himself comfortable on the lap that Esja had just criss-crossed her legs to make for him.

"I guess you have your answer," I said.

"Thanks, Ingrid," she said. But then she gave my shoulder a little shove. "Now, you should go. Dance with your boyfriend."

"Because he might be gone tomorrow?" I said wistfully. It had been meant as a joke, although even I had to admit it wasn't a particularly funny one.

But to my surprise, Esja was shaking her head. "No, I don't think so. I told you before, I think I can see how the future will grow out of the past now, right?"

"Yeah?" I said.

"Yeah, and I have to say, when I look into your future and Thorbjorn's, I don't see all that many days apart," she said. "A few. But not all that many."

"Thank you, Esja," I said. She just smiled, then her turned attention to the cat in her lap who was looking for pets.

But as I crossed the village commons to pull my boyfriend away from bragging with his brothers and closer to the band playing the foot-stomping music, I truly hoped she was right.

A few days apart at a time I could handle.

But I longed for that future where it was not all that many.

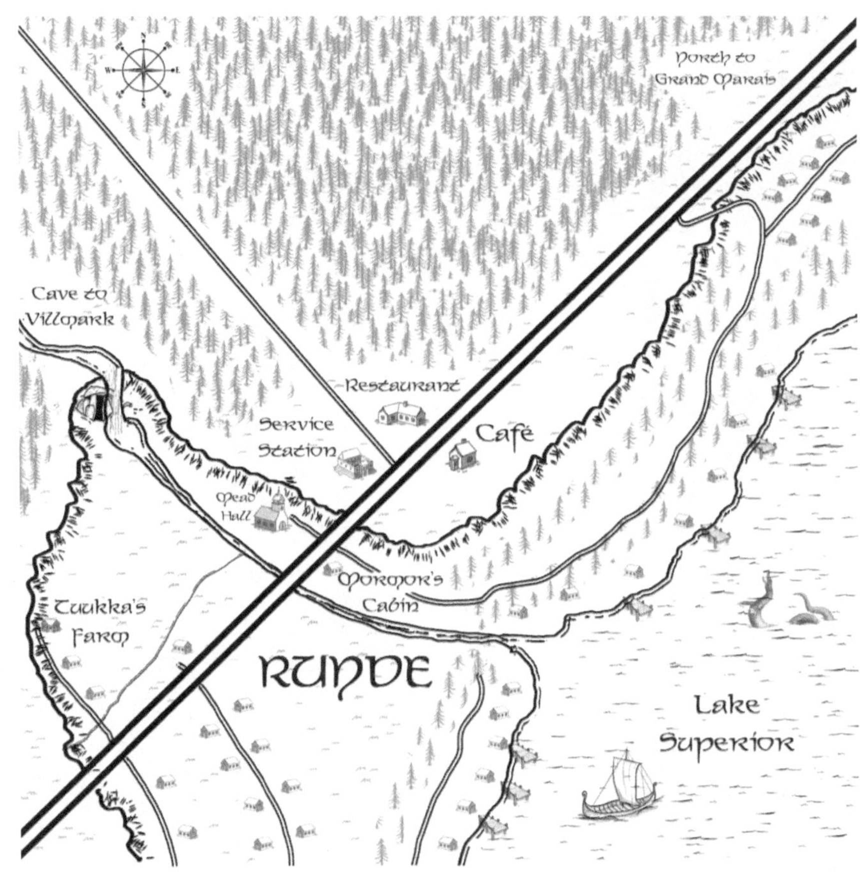

N
W E
S
North to
Grand Marais
Cave to
Villmark
Restaurant
Service
Station
Café
Mead
Hall
Mormor's
Cabin
Tuukka's
Farm
RUNDE
Lake
Superior

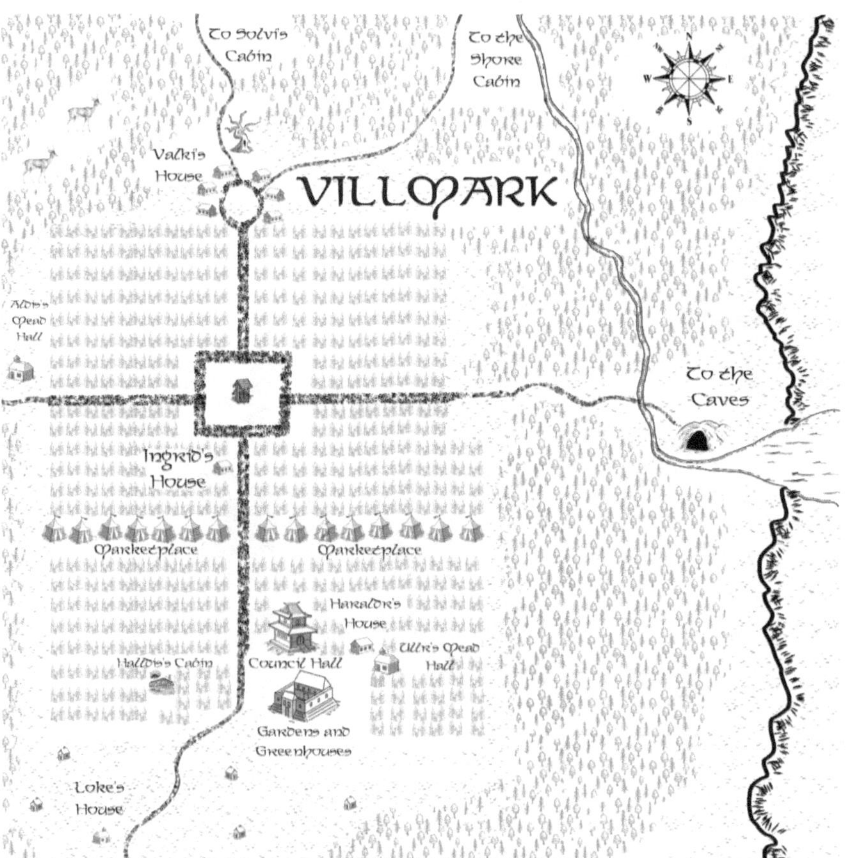
To Solvi's Cabin
To the Shore Cabin
Valki's House
VILLMARK
Aldi's Mead Hall
To the Caves
Ingrid's House
Marketplace
Marketplace
Haraldr's House
Ullr's Mead Hall
Halldis's Cabin
Council Hall
Gardens and Greenhouses
Loke's House
N
S
E
W

haven for ghosts. But what Ingrid senses just might be more than a mere haunting.

It might, in fact, be something more magical than that. Something that only she as a volva can face.

Snare in the Blind Alley, the fifteenth book in **The Viking Witch Mystery Series**!

THE WITCHES THREE
COZY MYSTERIES

In case you missed it, check out **Charm School**, the first book in the complete **Witches Three Cozy Mystery Series**!

Amanda Clarke thinks of herself as perfectly ordinary in every way. Just a small-town girl who serves breakfast all day in a little diner nestled next to the highway, nothing but dairy farms for miles around. She fits in there.

But then an old woman she never met dies, and Amanda was named in her will. Now Amanda packs a bag and heads to the big city, to Miss Zenobia Weekes' Charm School for Exceptional Young Ladies. And it's not in just any neighborhood. No, she finds herself on Summit Avenue in St. Paul, a street lined with gorgeous old houses, the former homes of lumber barons, railroad millionaires, even the writer F. Scott Fitzgerald. Why, Amanda can practically hear the jazz music still playing across the decades.

Scratch that. The music really, literally, still plays in the backyard of the charm school. Because the house stretches across time itself. Without a witch to protect this tear in the fabric of the world, anything can spill over. Like music.

Or like murder.

Charm School, the first book in the complete **Witches Three Cozy Mystery Series!**

THE WEAL & WOE BOOKSHOP
WITCH MYSTERIES

In case you missed it, check out **The Teashop Terror**, the first book in the complete **Weal & Woe Bookshop Witch Mystery Series**!

No one knows more about every branch of magic than Tabitha Greene. She devoted years to studying the most esoteric texts, hunting down the most obscure source materials, and deciphering the most cryptic ancient scrolls. But her career in academia hits a dead end when no wizard will take her on as an apprentice.

Just because, despite being descended from two long and prestigious lines of witches, her attempts to actually perform any magic always fail. Often spectacularly.

But no more college means no more dorm life. And no magical skills means no real job skills, at least, not in the witchy world. And a life spent moving from school to school every few months was a life without real friendships. She finds herself alone with nowhere to go.

Then an uncle she barely remembers offers her a summer job, running his bookstore over the summer. The Weal and Woe Bookstore, located in a magical pocket world within a block of buildings just north of the old Mill District of Minneapolis, Minnesota.

Not exactly the pinnacle of all her hopes and dreams. But it's just for one summer, right?

Or so Tabitha tells herself. But unbeknownst to her, the Weal and Woe Bookstore is about to change her life.

The Teashop Terror, the first book in the complete **Weal & Woe Bookshop Witch Mystery Series**!

ALSO FROM RATATOSKR PRESS

The Ritchie and Fitz Sci-Fi Murder Mysteries starts with **Murder on the Intergalactic Railway**.

For Murdina Ritchie, acceptance at the Oymyakon Foreign Service Academy means one last chance at her dream of becoming a diplomat for the Union of Free Worlds. For Shackleton Fitz IV, it represents his last chance not to fail out of military service entirely.

Strange that fate should throw them together now, among the last group of students admitted after the start of the semester. They had once shared the strongest of friendships. But that all ended a long time ago.

But when an insufferable but politically important woman turns up murdered, the two agree to put their differences aside and work together to solve the case.

Because the murderer might strike again. But more importantly, solving a murder would just have to impress the dour colonel who clearly thinks neither of them belong at his academy.

Murder on the Intergalactic Railway, the first book in **The Ritchie**

and Fitz Sci-Fi Murder Mysteries, available everywhere books are sold.

FREE EBOOK!

Like exclusive, free content?

If you'd like to receive "A Collection of Witchy Prequels", a free collection of short story prequels to the Witches Three Cozy Mystery and Viking Witch Mystery series, as well as other free stories throughout the year, go to my website CateMartin.com to subscribe to my newsletter! This eBook is exclusively for newsletter subscribers and will never be sold in stores. Check it out!

ABOUT THE AUTHOR

Cate Martin has written stories which have appeared in **Mystery, Crime and Mayhem** quarterly magazine as well as in the annual **Holiday Spectacular** Advent calendar of Christmas stories. She is also the author of three witch mystery series: **The Witches Three Cozy Mysteries**, and **The Viking Witch Mysteries** and **The Weal and Woe Bookshop Witch Mysteries**. She currently lives in Minneapolis, Minnesota. You can learn more about her work at CateMartin.com.

ALSO BY CATE MARTIN

The Witches Three Cozy Mystery Series
Charm School
Work Like a Charm
Third Time is a Charm
Old World Charm
Charm his Pants Off
Charm Offensive

The Witches Three Cozy Mysteries Books 1-3
The Witches Three Cozy Mysteries Books 4-6

The Viking Witch Mystery Series
Body at the Crossroads
Death Under the Bridge
Murder on the Lake
Killing in the Village Commons
Bloodshed in the Forest
Corpse in the Mead Hall
Slaying on the Lake Shore
Bones by the Forest Road
Sacrifice Behind the Falls
Body Under the Café
Assassination in the Glade
Bewitchment After the Storm
Predator in the Lanes
Threat From the North
Snare in the Blind Alley

Ashes Beneath the Tree (available July 14, 2026 direct from me or August 11, 2026 in stores everywhere)

The Viking Witch Mysteries Books 1-3

The Viking Witch Mysteries Books 4-6

The Viking Witch Mysteries Books 7-9

The Weal & Woe Bookshop Witch Mystery Series

The Teashop Terror

The Salon & Spa Scandal

The Bookseller Blunder

The Entrepreneur Enigma

The Novelty Shop Nightmare

The Courtyard Conundrum

Short Story Collections

Bubbly, Bicycles and Brides

The Dorothy Lundegaard Mysteries

Fruitcake, Festivities and Firelight